D0953469

Almost Home

Books by

JOAN BAUER

x x x

Almost Home

Backwater

Best Foot Forward

Close to Famous

Hope Was Here

Peeled

Rules of the Road

Squashed

Stand Tall

Stick

Thwonk

JOAN BAUER

Almost Home

VIKING
An Imprint of Penguin Group (USA) Inc.

VIKING
Published by the Penguin Group
Penguin Young Readers Group, 345 Hudson Street, New York, New York 10014, U.S.A.
Penguin Group (Canada), 90 Eglinton Avenue East, Suite 700, Toronto, Ontario, Canada M4P 2Y3
(a division of Pearson Penguin Canada Inc.)
Penguin Books Ltd, 80 Strand, London WC2R 0RL, England
Penguin Ireland, 25 St Stephen's Green, Dublin 2, Ireland (a division of Penguin Books Ltd)
Penguin Group (Australia), 250 Camberwell Road, Camberwell, Victoria 3124, Australia
(a division of Pearson Australia Group Pty Ltd)
Penguin Books India Pvt Ltd, 11 Community Centre, Panchsheel Park, New Delhi—110 017, India
Penguin Group (NZ), 67 Apollo Drive, Rosedale, Auckland 0632, New Zealand
(a division of Pearson New Zealand Ltd.)
Penguin Books (South Africa) (Pty) Ltd, 24 Sturdee Avenue, Rosebank, Johannesburg 2196, South Africa
Penguin Books Ltd, Registered Offices: 80 Strand, London WC2R 0RL, England

First published in the United States of America by Viking,
a division of Penguin Young Readers Group, 2012

5 7 9 10 8 6

LIBRARY OF CONGRESS CATALOGING-IN-PUBLICATION DATA
Bauer, Joan, date–
Almost home / by Joan Bauer.
p. cm.
Summary: Sixth-grader Sugar and her mother lose their beloved house and experience
the harsh world of homelessness.
ISBN 978-0-670-01289-3 (hardcover)
[1. Homeless persons—Fiction. 2. Mothers and daughters—Fiction.] I. Title.
PZ7.B32615Al 2012 [Fic]—dc23 2011050483

Printed in U.S.A. Set in Fairfield Book design by Nancy Brennan

For my sisters, Barb and Karen, with much love

× × ×

WITH SPECIAL THANKS TO: Barbara Dwyer, MSW, who provided a rich understanding of foster care, children at risk, and the unstoppable power of resilience.

Beth Fuller, family therapist, who helped me see how broken families can move toward wholeness.

James Nelson, bass player supreme, who taught me the realities of musicians, bands, and the fine art of collaboration.

Dr. John Morehead, veterinarian and overall great guy, who helped me explore the heart and the potential of a frightened, abused dog and a child's responsibility to care for him.

Regina Hayes, my editor, who knew how to bring this story home.

Evan, my husband, who supports in every conceivable way; Jean, my daughter, an invaluable early reader; and JoAnn, Rita, Laura, Mickey, Kally, Donna, Catrina, and Chris—true friends who believe.

1

MR. BENNETT WALKED into room 212 carrying a plastic bag. He smoothed his sweatshirt that read DEATH TO STEREOTYPES, tucked Claus his rubber chicken under his arm, raised one eyebrow, and jumped on his desk. He opened the bag, lifted a loaf of bread into the air and shouted, "Sell it to me."

He threw the bread on the desk.

Peyton Crawler let his eyes go back into his head like he'd been dead for years. Harper Wilhelm hollered, "It's good for you."

Everyone in sixth-grade English groaned. Mr. Bennett shook his head. "It has to be more than that."

"You're hungry," Katie Nesbitt said.

Mr. B shrugged.

I see where he's going. I raised my hand. "Do you like toast?"

Peyton Crawler smirked. "That's stupid."

Go back to being dead, Peyton.

"As a matter of fact," Mr. B announced, "I love toast."

I pressed in. "With butter and jam?"

He pulled down his orange wool hat and grinned. "Strawberry jam."

I had what I needed. I ran up and grabbed the bread. "Then I can tell you, that this bread"—I looked at the label—"Aunt Fanny's Homemade Honey Bread, makes *the* best toast in the universe."

Mr. Bennett jumped off the desk and looked at the price. "It's expensive."

"It costs more because it's better," I told him. "And you can freeze half of it, and only use it when you want toast. It'll make you so happy, you won't be able to stand it."

He walked to the huge B that hung on the wall behind his desk—the Great B, he called it. "Sold." He slammed Claus on the desk (rubber chickens don't mind). "Why did she sell me?"

Kids looked at each other, clueless. Mr. B twirled Claus in the air. "These are golden lessons from my checkered career in advertising. *Think.* What did Sugar do?" Mr. Bennett was in advertising for fifteen years and made real decent money, but he gave it all up to teach sixth grade.

Katie raised her hand. "She had to learn about you before she could sell you the bread."

"That's right. She persuaded me. She formed an argument to convince me." He stood in front of the smaller B on the wall—the not-so-great B. "So, when you are trying to sell someone something—an idea, a loaf of bread, whatever—find out what the person is about."

Mr. Bennett held up an ad with a picture of a cool-looking singer standing by a piano. "What's wrong with this picture?" he asked us.

Simon said, "There's nothing wrong with it."

"Look closer," Mr. Bennett suggested.

Carrie said, "I love her dress."

Mr. Bennett looked at the ad. "Nice dress."

I said, "She's holding a cigarette in her left hand. You don't see it at first."

Mr. Bennett nodded. "And why is that?"

"They're trying to show that smoking is cool," Carrie said.

"They're trying to manipulate you," Mr. Bennett said. "Your mind takes in the photo—you don't notice the cigarette at first, if ever, but it's there."

"They want us to smoke," I said.

"That's right."

And my mind went to Mr. Leeland, my father, who looked so good in so many ways, being handsome and funny and seeming to love life, but in his left hand there was always a losing hand.

"Persuasion is an art. It can be misused or it can be powerful. Tonight, I want all of you, including the dead among us"—Mr. B threw Claus into Peyton's lap—"to write a stirring paragraph on one way you have seen persuasion misused—an advertising campaign, something on the Internet, something in your life. Specifics are found on thegreatbknowsall.com."

I wondered if I should write about Mr. Leeland and how he always persuaded Reba to believe he was going to come through for us.

"I will read the best three out loud in class, so work excessively hard on this."

I wouldn't want anything about Mr. Leeland read out loud.

Harper Wilhelm was giving me her evil eye like she knew all my secrets. I smiled and walked past her. Reba says it's good to smile around people who don't like you—it makes you stronger. I beamed a big one in Harper's direction; she looked disgusted and left the room. I walked up to Mr. B. He was exactly my height—five feet four inches. His ski cap had dogs on it.

"Mr. B, I've got something real personal I want to write about, but I wouldn't want the class to hear it."

He adjusted his hat. "Well, make it so good, it will kill me not to read it out loud."

I grinned. "I'll try." I stood there because I didn't want to go home. I wished I could tell him all that was happening at my house. "I'm not sure how to start writing about it."

He leaned Claus against his coffee mug. "Writing about personal things isn't easy, Sugar. Try breaking it up into small, manageable pieces."

Small and manageable was not what my life was like.

He looked at me. "Are you okay?"

That depends on how you define okay.

x x x

I walked home with Meesha Moy, my best friend. Her life wasn't small and manageable either. Even when we were a block from her house, we could hear the sound of bad accordion music carried on the wind. Meesha stopped walking and shook her head. Two months ago, her family had to rent out her room to Mr. Denton who played, or tried to play, the accordion. Meesha had to sleep on the couch in the TV room. Her dad got sick and the bills were killing them. We had a lot in common, except that Meesha's dad couldn't work because he was sick. Mr. Leeland didn't work because he was a gambler.

We haven't had to rent out a room . . . yet.

The bad accordion music got louder; a dog started howling. Meesha looked like she could start howling, too, but Reba taught me to be grateful no matter what. I looked up at the blue sky. "It's a pretty day, huh?"

Meesha glared at me. "If it was raining, he wouldn't be practicing on the porch."

I nodded and headed down Pleasant Street, my street, working hard at my gratitude. Reba was always telling me, "You take the *G-R* out of gratitude and you've got attitude."

Only once did I mention that attitude's got three *T*'s, not two.

"I'm teaching you enduring concepts for living," she snapped. "Not spelling."

Chester, our postman, was pushing his cart down the street. My grandpa, King Cole, was a mailman until the day he died. "Mail tells a story," he always told me. "A good mail carrier knows what's going on in every house on his route. They know who's paying their bills on time, they know who's late."

Chester looked at me with sympathy and handed me a stack of envelopes all marked URGENT. I hate that word. Only one was addressed to me, or halfway at any rate. It had curlicue writing.

> Sugar Booger Cole
> 14 Pleasant St.
> Round Lake, MO

I sighed. Sugar isn't the easiest name to be slapped with, I'll tell you. I was supposed to get named Susannah. I was supposed to get born in a hospital, too, but my whole life started as one big surprise when I got born in the back of a Chevy in the parking lot of the Sugar Shack in Baton Rouge in a rainstorm so bad, my parents couldn't make it to the hospital. When I popped out and Reba saw the Sugar Shack sign, she felt it was a sign from God; right then I got my name. At least God told her to stop at Sugar. Sugar Shack Cole would have been a chore to live with. As for Mr. Leeland, he got the thrill of helping me get born, and believe me, he hasn't done squat to help since then.

But I was grateful. As soon as I could write, I sent a note to the Chevrolet company in Detroit, Michigan, and thanked them for making such good backseats that a baby could get born and be okay. That company cared so much, they wrote me back and said that although many babies had been born in Chevrolet backseats over the years, I was the first one they knew of named Sugar.

Reba says part of why I'm on this earth is to bring a little sweetness into people's lives. "And sweet doesn't mean stupid," she says. "Sweet doesn't mean weak. I'm not talking kittens wearing sun hats either. I'm talking kindness. You go out there, Sugar Mae Cole, and show 'em what it means to be sweet."

I threw the Sugar Booger envelope into the garbage and walked up the path to our house. The yellow paint was cracked and our porch needed repair, but we had hanging flowerpots that made up for some of that. Reba was sitting on the porch in a white chair with her pink phone to her ear, clutching the little silver bell on the necklace Mr. Leeland had given her last year right before she kicked him out for the umpteenth time. Mr. Leeland got it in Atlanta and called it her southern bell. Reba's big desire is to be a fine Southern belle, which is kind of like being a lady on steroids.

When Reba clutched that bell, it meant she was ready to pop off and working hard to find her graces.

"Why yes," she said into her pink phone, "yes, I know, and I'm terribly sorry we're late again." Her voice went deep Southern now, pouring the words out like hot butterscotch melting vanilla ice cream. "But I'm struggling as it is to pay the rent. Surely, sir, you understand that I can't manage the late fee." Reba clung to that bell like it was a lifesaver. She closed her eyes. "Why, yes, I hope we will be able to resolve this soon as well. You have a nice day now." She flipped her phone shut and shouted, "Honking, skinflint moron! If his brains were dynamite, he couldn't blow his nose!"

I wanted to know more about the late fee, but I decided not to ask. King Cole always told me, "If you've got a good, fair question and you ask it at the wrong time, what do you get?"

Answer: "In trouble."

I kissed Reba on the head and went inside to start my paragraph on bad persuasion.

It's always good when homework can help you manage a part of your life.

2

THERE ARE PEOPLE *in our lives we cannot trust.*

One of those people in my life is my father.

Is there Gorilla Glue for fathers, I wonder?

Duct tape to keep one together?

I remember so much and wish I didn't.

All the fights about him borrowing money and never paying it back.

All the times he'd play cards with me for money.

I was little, but he always won.

There was a strange look in his eyes when that happened.

Sometimes he'd disappear and not come back for the longest time.

He had the gift of persuasion.

His voice sounded like he meant every word,

His eyes would fill with love,

And it was hard to believe he didn't mean what he said,
But he didn't.
I've learned a lot having a father like this.
One of the big lessons is that you learn about people
Not just by the words they say, or the promises they make,
But by what they do.
I want to be the kind of person who does what I say I'll do.
I want people to know they can trust me.

Mr. B said to write a paragraph, but the words of this poem poured out of me from some secret place. He was going to have to adjust.

There were probably lots of poems to write about my father.

My grandma, Mr. Leeland's mother, used to say, "You be respectful of your father, Sugar, for he's been through harder times than you know."

I didn't know what those hard times were, other than all the times he lost money gambling. I asked King Cole how you respect someone you don't trust.

"Now, that's one the great minds have been wrestling with for ages. It's not the easiest thing to do. They're all agreed on that."

"Did they come up with an answer a kid can understand?"

"It just so happens they did. Everyone alive has good parts and bad parts to them. Some people work hard to develop the good parts, and others work hard on the bad. I think we can respect a person's potential—what they could be—but we don't have to like it if they're acting the wrong way. Do you know what I mean?"

"Like they've got good things inside they don't know how to get at?"

"That's right—they're in a locked drawer."

"And they can't find the key."

He grinned and wrote that down in his notebook. "That's good truth, isn't it? And I'm giving you full credit for this one." He wrote some more. " 'This concept was inspired by Sugar Mae Cole, one of the great minds of our time.' "

I laughed. "I am not."

"It's my book. I say what I believe."

He put that in chapter two of his autobiography, *Upon These Truths I Stand.* King Cole wasn't a real king, but he always felt he had royalty inside. I missed him bad. I did a shadowbox of him in school for inspiration week. I had him standing by a sunset; the sign by the road read SOME SUNS WILL NEVER SET.

"What does that mean?" Peyton Crawler asked it not too nice.

"It means he had so much sunshine in him, it filled up the sky."

"I don't get it."

"I can't help that."

King Cole was on chapter ten of his autobiography when he died. I've read every chapter except number three, "Women I Have Known and Sometimes Loved." I'd just gotten to the part when he met the beautiful Marla Monroe at a 7-Eleven in Baton Rogue when Reba yanked it from me.

"Can I at least read it when I'm older?"

"No you cannot."

I don't know where she hid that chapter. I've looked everywhere for it.

The last thing he ever told me was, "It's not fair, but sometimes a kid has to act older than their age. If that happens to you, pray hard about what to do. You hear me?"

"Yessir."

He took my hand. "You're going to fall down in this life—everybody does. But you be the kind of person who doesn't stay down for long. Get back on your feet and keep going no matter what."

"I will."

When he died, I wrote him a thank-you note. I wish I hadn't waited to do it. I made a copy of the note at the library, crying at the Xerox machine.

"Are you all right?" the librarian asked me.

"My grandpa died."

"Oh, my dear." She picked up a vase with fresh flowers from the return desk and handed it to me. "These are for you."

Being this was a library, I wasn't sure if I had to return them, so I figured I'd better ask.

"They're for you to keep," she said.

That's something coming from a librarian.

I took them to the funeral home and put them near King Cole's coffin. He always said when his autobiography came out, it would be front and center at the four-day book table. Just about everything he told me was right, except that.

I put my thank-you note in his coffin before they closed it.

Dear King Cole,

I don't know how to thank you for everything you've done for me. I think every word you've ever spoken to me is in my heart, and I promise you I won't lose one of them. You took over raising me when my own daddy couldn't do it. You were happy when it didn't make sense, and you showed me how to love life and people. I don't know what I'm going to do without you, but I want you to know, I'm going to be the person you always saw in me. I don't know how, but I am.

I love you, Grandpa, and I'm going to miss you like crazy, but I'm going to picture you dancing up in heaven having the time of your life. Not everybody gets to live with a true person who's also a king, but I got to. I promise I won't take it for granted.
XOXOXOXOXOXOXOXOXOXOXOXOXOXOX

Sugar

When we got home from the funeral, I took out my journal and wrote, *Today, I'm going to have to act older than I am.*

X X X

I headed across the Iversons' backyard to the path by the ridge that led to Mrs. Pittman's house and my really odd job. It wasn't easy getting this job. Mrs. Pittman called my school looking for "a youngster with a good attitude who can do rudimentary tasks." Three eighth-graders applied for it who probably knew what rudimentary meant. Me, I was in sixth grade and up for anything; I just needed to make some money.

"Why should I hire you over an eighth-grader?" Mrs. Pittman asked me.

"Because eighth-graders don't always do what they're told, ma'am. I'm young and still respectful."

"See that you stay that way." And I got hired right there. I'm twelve now, and for the most part, I've stayed respectful.

I walked up the path to the old stone house. Leona, her housekeeper, was sweeping the porch.

"How is she today?" I asked.

Leona shook her head and went back to sweeping. I

walked in the front door, wiped my feet on the welcome mat that read GO AWAY, and walked past her collection of cuckoo clocks. It was exactly three o'clock, and all the cuckoos went crazy.

Cuckoo, cuckoo.

That really fit around here. I knocked on Mrs. Pittman's bedroom door. "It's me."

"The children," she said, "are hungry."

I opened the door. "Right." I picked up the bag of bread pieces.

She looked out the window at the lake. "Now, you know what to tell them."

"That you're sorry you haven't been able to spend any time with them, but it doesn't mean you don't care." This is where Meesha lost it when she subbed for me; I had a sore throat so bad I couldn't eat.

"That's right. And you've got the food?"

I held up the bag of bread pieces.

She grinned. "And be sure you look for Bessie."

"I will."

Mrs. Pittman believed that Bessie, the sister of the Loch Ness monster, a famous monster in Scotland, was living at the bottom of Round Lake just waiting to be discovered. "Monsters know how to hide," she told me.

"You have to watch for the signs to see if they're moving. Look for shadows, look for any movement on top of the water."

"Okay." I headed outside, walked down the path to the little lake, and threw some bread into the water. The ducks swam fast to get it.

"Look, you guys, I'm getting paid to tell you this. Mrs. Pittman says she hasn't been able to spend any time with you because she's been sick, but it doesn't mean she doesn't care. This is from her." I tossed more bread in the water and a dozen ducks went for it, causing ripples everywhere.

I sat down on the bank and watched the surface of the lake. Was there a great sea monster swimming down deep? The first day I came to work for Mrs. Pittman, she told me about Bessie.

"She's waiting," Mrs. Pittman explained.

"Waiting for what?"

"Waiting for her close-up. She's playing us now."

I met an official monster once. He wasn't in a lake, he was at my front door.

"Where's your father?" he snarled.

"He's not here."

The man had big hands. He cracked his knuckles. "Where is he?"

"I . . . I don't know. He only stays with us sometimes. I haven't seen him for—"

"You tell your old man this. You tell him I came by and I'm going to keep doing that until we get paid all the money he owes us. You think you can remember that?"

You think I can ever forget that, mister?

I threw the rest of the bread in the water. "Are you there, Bessie?"

What do monsters eat anyway?

Bread?

Ducks?

Or maybe sixth-graders?

3

MR. B READ my poem on bad persuasion a couple of times and shook his head. I figured that meant I had failed, and it was a rough blow after emptying my heart about my mess of a father.

He looked up at me. I took a huge breath.

"You did it, Sugar. You did me in. It will kill me not to read this to the class."

I broke out in a grin.

"Have you talked to someone about your dad? This isn't easy stuff."

"I've talked to my grandpa." *And now you.*

"And that helped?"

"Talking to him always helped." I mentioned the locked drawer.

"Do me a favor. Write about that drawer sometime."

I wasn't sure my brain had that kind of range, but I said I'd try.

"I appreciate how hard you try, Sugar."

He twirled Claus in the air after he said it.

I never want to leave sixth grade. Ever.

I mentioned this to my friend Woody, as we were walking to the cafeteria. "There's more to life than sixth grade," he said.

"I can't imagine having a better teacher than Mr. B. I mean, how many rubber chickens are there in education?"

He nodded. "Claus might be the only one."

That's when Harper Wilhelm crashed against me, giggling. I dropped my books. She grinned. I felt my face turn red, but I just smiled bigger at her. Woody put his face close to hers. "Nice imitation of a truck, Harper." Then he helped me pick up my books.

My poem about Mr. Leeland landed in the corner. Woody headed for it.

"Don't read that! It's personal!"

Wrong thing to say. Harper scooped it up.

I screamed. "Give it to me, Harper!"

I tried grabbing it as she read out loud, "'There are people in our lives we cannot trust. One of those people in my life is my father.'" She was laughing and I hated her. I didn't care what Reba said about being sweet. "'Is there Gorilla Glue for fathers, I wonder?'" She smirked.

I felt my face turn purple. Woody grabbed the paper from her. So many kids were watching. Now everybody knew. Staying in sixth grade forever didn't sound like a great idea anymore.

Mr. B walked up. He didn't usually get angry, but he was now. He pointed a finger at Harper. "That was a cheap shot, Harper." He looked around. "Just so all of you know, that was the best poem in the class. It took great courage to write it, and don't any of you make fun of something that rings so deep and true." He stared at Harper, who was looking down. "I was about to take a break, but I'd much rather take you to the principal's office."

"For what?" she shouted.

"For inappropriate, unkind, and asinine behavior."

Kids gasped at the *A* word.

"Any questions?" Mr. B demanded.

Kids looked down, except me. I looked right at Mr. B like he was an angel swooping down to save me. He nodded and took Harper to the principal.

Meesha Moy walked up. "He should have used handcuffs."

I tried to smile, but I just felt like I'd been invaded; all my pain, all my secrets.

"I'm sorry that happened," Woody muttered.

Marna, my science partner, said, "She's mean, Sugar. Don't let it stick."

A few months ago, Harper had written a mean poem about me. That girl can rhyme. I showed it to Reba.

"I think deep down Miss Harper Wilhelm doesn't like herself much," she told me, "and if she can concentrate on disliking you, she doesn't have to face her own badness."

We took the poem, put it in a bag of garbage with smelly eggshells and old oatmeal, and threw it in the trash.

"If you're inclined to go back searching for those words, remember what you'll have to dig through to find them," Reba told me.

I ate oatmeal for breakfast that whole week to let the concept sink in. Then I wrote Harper a thank-you note and taped it to her locker.

Dear Harper,

I know what you're doing and why you're doing it.

I feel real sorry for you. Thank you for this important lesson I will never forget.

Sugar Mae Cole

She didn't stop hating me, but she did stop writing poems, at least for a while, and if she sent that Sugar Booger envelope, it's where it belongs—in the garbage.

I guess if you look hard enough, there's always something to be grateful for.

x x x

The man from the bank had small eyes and a red face; he was sitting at our kitchen table when I got home from school. Reba's face was paler than usual.

"You go on to your room, Sugar," she directed.

I sat at the table, too. I wasn't leaving my mother alone with this guy.

Reba shot me her *obey now* look. I put the oldest expression I had on my face. "I'm staying."

"It appears, Mr. Bergen, my daughter will be joining us."

The bank man ignored me. "Here's the thing, Miz Cole. You've not paid your full monthly mortgage payment for five months now. Add onto that the loan your husband took out against the house."

What loan? I looked at Reba, who was looking down.

The bank man shook his head; his extra chin jiggled. "Those late fees pile up faster than manure in a stable." He laughed. We didn't.

"My husband, Mr. Leeland, has had some difficulty securing the money to pay back the loan, and I had no idea things had gotten to this point. But I assure you—"

Was she kidding? Trusting Mr. Leeland to pay back money was like trusting a dog to watch your food.

"Miz Cole, we've talked to you about this over the phone for some time now, we've sent you letters. This cannot be a surprise to you. You're in the hole big-time, ma'am."

I didn't know anything about loans or what Mr. Leeland did, but I wasn't going to let him know that.

Reba bit her lip. "Mr. Bergen, since my father's passing one year ago, I've done everything I could to hold on to our home."

"These are tough times, Miz Cole, but People's Trust isn't running a charity."

People's *Trust*?

Give me a break.

Reba stood up and stomped her foot. I did the exact same thing.

The bank man leaned back in his chair. "I know you're suffering because of the death of your father, and we've given you all the breaks we can. There's no way around it, you have to be out."

I couldn't believe what I was hearing. We had to leave our house?

The bank man pushed some papers toward Reba. "This here is what you sign that says you agree to these terms." He handed her a pen.

Reba breathed out hard like she'd been hit in the stomach.

"Just sign here, Miz Cole." Reba took the pen.

"Don't sign it," I said.

The bank man didn't like that. "You're a feisty one."

"She shouldn't sign it if she hasn't read it and understood everything it says." I added "sir" to be respectful. That advice was in King Cole's book, chapter seven—"Don't Let the Scumbags Get You Down." I'd memorized a lot of this book.

The bank man fixed his small eyes on me. "And how old are you?"

Reba slapped the pen on the table. "Old enough to not be pushed around. I'll be having my attorney look at these papers and we'll be getting back to you."

"Miz Cole, do you realize the gravity of this situation?"

Reba gripped her silver bell. She got laid off four months ago from her full-time job at Len Norris Toyota and had been cleaning houses to make ends meet, although the ends weren't meeting. "Mr. Bergen, I expect you should be going."

"Miz Cole, you're making a big—"

"*Now,* sir."

Just then thunder boomed and rain poured down. I was glad he was going to get wet. Reba put her head in her hands. I waited for her to say something, but she didn't. I looked at the papers. I knew it was right not to sign them, but King Cole never wrote a word about what to do when you're getting kicked out.

A big wind blew our screen door shut. "What kind of loan did you give Mr. Leeland?"

She gulped. "It was against what's been paid off on the house."

"What does that mean?"

"Mr. Leeland is going to do the right thing by us."

"No, he's not, Reba."

"You show great disrespect for your father, miss."

"He shows great disrespect for us!"

She walked out of the room. I followed her.

"What are we going to do, Reba?"

She took an enormous breath. "We're going to find the way through this." She closed her baby-blue eyes. "I have to think."

You do that. I have to think, too.

I marched upstairs and sat at my desk that began its life as a door. King Cole found it on the street, sanded it down, and painted it yellow, my favorite color. I opened the box of my least favorite note cards.

I would never send this note, but it felt good to write.

Dear Mr. Bergen,

I'm young, but I know about monsters. I've dealt with them before and I'll do it again. Get your fat hands off our house and leave us alone!

Yours very truly,

Sugar Mae Cole

I took out another card and wrote,

Dear Mr. Leeland,

If you were ever looking for a time to do the right thing, this is it. Reba's counting on you, and me . . . well . . . I'm just hoping.

Sugar

4

I WAS SITTING by Mrs. Pittman's bed singing "You'll Never Walk Alone." It was her second favorite song, next to "Happy Days Are Here Again," and I was moving into the big finish, where I stood up and sang about how even though your dreams get tossed and torn, you've got to keep on walking.

"Tossed and *blown*," Mrs. Pittman corrected me.

I sang that part over, then I got serious and closed my eyes. I wasn't the best singer (I could mostly carry a tune), but I knew how to put my heart into a song. I sang about how you've got to walk on through the wind and the rain and do this with hope in your heart, which is a lot to manage, in my opinion.

This could be my theme song.

"Sing it, child!" Mrs. Pittman waved her hands in the air.

My hands went up as I finished. Mrs. Pittman and Leona applauded. Leona brushed a tear from her eye, which was something, since Leona mostly had one expression—irritated.

Mrs. Pittman said, "I think that's the best rendition I've ever heard."

I smiled. I guess when you start living a song, you can really sing it.

"And I liked what you did with your voice at the end. It's very important to end big and leave 'em wanting more."

"Yes, ma'am."

She grinned. "That got my heart going. God knows I need it. Get my wheelchair, Leona. I need to see the children."

Leona brought it over and helped Mrs. Pittman into the chair.

"You want a blanket or something?" I asked.

"Absolutely not."

Leona wheeled her outside, down the lawn to the lake. All the ducks looked up and started swimming toward her.

She raised her hands. "Children. Receive your queen!"

The ducks quacked and waddled right up to her. She tossed bread chunks at them. "I've missed you," she said. Her face was beaming. One little duck quacked very loud. "Yes, I know. I know," Mrs. Pittman said.

"We should go back in," Leona grumbled.

"Not yet. Wheel me to the edge."

"Oh, Mrs. P!"

"Leona . . ."

Leona wheeled her closer, not understanding, but I knew. I walked over to the wheelchair. "Do you see her, Mrs. Pittman? Do you see Bessie?"

And it was like a movie moment when all the animals were still and there was no wind and the lake shone like a diamond. Mrs. Pittman pointed to a small ripple in the middle of the lake.

"There she is!"

I looked.

"She's gone deep, but she's there." Mrs. Pittman touched my arm. "Sugar Mae Cole, I give you the ability to see monsters in the deep and to not be afraid when they surface."

X X X

I put the fifteen dollars from Mrs. Pittman in my suitcase. I had exactly two hundred and thirty-seven dollars in this case. I'm an excellent saver. I ran my hand over the money, closed the case and headed downstairs.

I handed it to Reba. "Here. You can have it."

She took my hand. "I appreciate that, but you keep your money."

"I'm part of this family. I can help!"

Reba sat down on the couch that she'd re-covered herself with flowered fabric. "Sugar, this is the sweetest thing, but nothing within me could ever take your money."

"But, Reba—"

"We're going to be all right." She stood up and squared her shoulders like Southern women do. "I'll figure things out. Don't you worry."

I almost believed her.

A note was on my pillow that night.

Dear Sugar,

Your kindness in offering me your hard-earned money so blessed my heart. I've spent the rest of the day thinking about all the riches I have and topping that list is you. We're going to find the best way through this. I promise you that.

Sleep sweet, my girl.

With love and thanks,

Reba

I pulled down my window shade and crawled into bed.

Where in the world could we find a new place to live in two weeks?

X X X

I had a long night. I kept getting out of bed and walking through the house, remembering when we moved here after Reba and Mr. Leeland got divorced the first time. I was in second grade, and King Cole and Reba scraped together all they had and bought this house together. We were so proud to have our own little place. We painted the front door emerald green. It wasn't the best paint job, but I remember going through that door and feeling my life was fresh and new and all the shadows from Mr. Leeland's gambling were behind us. King Cole and I painted the wooden fence white and we fixed the cement steps. Reba and I planted peonies in the garden, and she repaired the rips in the screen door with clear nail polish. Mr. Leeland lived with us a few times, but he never stayed for long. He only cared if there was food and beer in the refrigerator, but me, Reba, and King Cole took care of this house with everything we had.

How could we be losing it?

But Reba always told me, things look better in the morning.

Morning came eventually. The sun was shining, dew drops glistened on the windows.

Something to be thankful for.

I had to write.

Dear God,

Thank you for sending the sun and the dew this morning. I needed that. A pot of money on the front porch wouldn't hurt either.

Ha Ha.

I hope all is well with you.

Yours very truly,

Sugar Mae Cole

5

I WAS WAITING for Reba in the parking lot of Real World Food. I'd just as soon be home, but Reba said tough luck, wait. I had a science experiment that Marna and I were supposed to be doing. We were going to make water glow by breaking open a yellow highlighter pen and removing the felt. There were some other steps, too, but we had failed the first one. Marna broke open the pen and got yellow dye on both our shirts. She said her mother was going to kill her and this was not a hypothesis. Reba said, "Well, yellow is your favorite color."

I didn't want to think about glowing water right now. I put down my green bag and sat on the bench.

"I don't want to hear any more lip from you!" a big man shouted to a girl a little younger than me. She was holding something in her arms wrapped in a blanket. A baby, I guess.

"But, Daddy!" she said, crying.

"I haven't got time for this!"

"But he needs me!" she shouted.

"Get in the car, Jenny!" he shouted and walked toward a big SUV. "Did you hear me?"

Everybody heard you, mister.

The girl Jenny was crying and looking around, desperate. She ran over to me.

"You like puppies, right?"

"What?"

She pulled down the blanket and what she was holding wasn't a baby, it was a little brown-and-white dog.

"You want him, right?"

"I can't have a dog."

"If you don't take him, my dad's taking him to the pound and they'll probably kill him."

The dog buried his nose in the blanket.

She put the dog in my arms. She was crying now. "My dad kicks him when he barks, so he's kind of nervous, but he's a good boy. Really." She put him in my arms. I felt him shake a little.

"Your dad kicks him?"

She looked down and nodded. "He's quiet, too. His name is Shush. Cute, huh? So, you take care of him and when he's older you tell him that Jenny always loved him and I'm sorry for all that happened." She was all-out crying now.

I held the puppy tight. I didn't think about how I would feed him or any of that. "I will," I told her. The girl ran off and got into an SUV. I held him close. "Nobody's going to kick you anymore." He nuzzled my hand. "You're going to have to do this exact thing to Reba's hand when she gets here. You're going to have to be the cutest dog in America."

The puppy whined.

"What a sweet puppy," a woman said. "What's his name?"

"Uh . . . Shush. . . ."

He wiggled as far under the blanket as he could.

She patted the blanket. "He's a shy little thing." Just then a car horn blasted and the dog jumped up. "Whoa," I said, gathering him back in the blanket. "It's okay." Actually, it wasn't close to okay. Reba was going to kill me, but I didn't think mentioning that to the dog right now would get us anywhere. Me, I like to know what's what, so I opened the blanket just a bit and said, "That noise you heard was a horn."

"I want the chocolate cereal, Mommy! I want it!

I want it!" A small child threw herself in front of the bench where I was sitting. The dog shook and the kid screamed. The girl's mother dragged her to the car.

The puppy was struggling to get free. I whispered, "That last noise you heard. That wasn't a horn—that was a brat."

I looked up to see Reba standing there.

"Who are you holding that dog for?"

"Well, the thing is . . ."

"Perhaps the better question is, what are you doing with a dog?"

I tried to explain. "I didn't know what to do, Reba. It happened so fast."

"Well, I know what to do." She took out her pink phone, pushed some buttons. "What's the closest animal shelter near Round Lake?"

I uncovered the dog so Reba could see all his adorableness. She turned away. "Could you connect me, please?"

Earlier in the day, I hadn't once thought how good it would feel to hold a puppy.

Reba waited, and waited, and waited some more, then snapped her pink phone shut. "They're closed."

Good.

The puppy put his paw on my hand and closed his eyes. *It would be good if you could do that to Reba.*

"His name is Shush and he's real quiet," I mentioned. "You want to hold him?"

She backed off. "I do not."

I cocked my head and the dog did, too.

"I left you alone for one minute, miss!"

"It was more like fifteen."

"Lord, give me strength."

We could both use some of that. I laid the puppy gently in Reba's arms. He put his little paw on her shoulder, put his head on her chest, and closed his eyes.

"I'm not looking at him, Sugar." She stared over at the bottle-recycling machine.

"He's like a baby," I mentioned.

She stood there for a long time. I picked up the two bags of groceries. The puppy made a tiny noise, and a smile started on Reba's face.

"I am not smiling," she said.

"Yes you are." I grinned. Grins were catching.

Shush made another noise, and Reba laughed despite herself. I knew I could keep him at least overnight.

If something can get Reba laughing, she's inclined to hold on to it. That's one of the reasons she still loves Mr. Leeland.

"We cannot afford a dog," she said.

"I know." I looked across the shopping center and saw the sign for Pet Universe. I took Shush in the blanket. "I'll be right back."

"Do not use your hard-earned money on—"

"I won't. I promise." I walked to Pet Universe. "I've been trained," I told Shush. "Watch this."

x x x

Sell it to me.

I walked up to a man who was putting dog food on a shelf.

"Excuse me, sir, but I was wondering if I could talk to you."

"Talk."

"Do you know what kind of food a puppy eats?"

He pointed to a shelf of bags that said FOR PUPPIES.

"Thanks." Shush put his paw on my shoulder and was sniffing the air. "Are you the manager of this store, sir?"

"That's Jim, in the back."

Jim in the back, I hope you've got more heart than this guy.

"Thank you." I walked back to Jim. "You must love dogs a lot to have this store," I said.

"I love dogs," Jim said. "I have three of my own."

"I have one."

"It's a good thing for a young person."

I took most of the blanket off Shush. "Do you see this puppy, sir?" I figured he did. "This puppy is going to be one of those helper dogs that goes to hospitals and shelters and makes people feel better."

Jim in the back scratched Shush's head. "Good for you."

"Yessir. And I was just given this dog, but I don't have any money for food, but I promise you, I am going to care for this puppy like it's my baby brother." I gulped.

Jim looked at me like I was crazy. Jim, you don't know the half of it.

"I was wondering, Mr. Jim, if you'd like to be a sponsor for this dog and give us some food. I'll mention Pet Universe every chance I get."

Jim looked at me strange.

"You can say you knew him when," I added.

He handed me a dog treat, and it wasn't that I wasn't grateful, but I needed more than that, and I told him so.

"I've been in the pet supply business for twenty-five years and this is a first," he told me.

I nodded.

"We really need your help, Mr. Jim. This is one special dog I'm holding."

He handed me a bag of puppy food and a box of dog biscuits. Then a lady handed me a dog toy in the shape of a bunny.

"Thank you. I'll come back and give you updates on how he's doing."

I headed out the door with Shush in one arm and the food in the other.

Mr. B, you're a true genius.

6

SHUSH SLEPT ON a towel by my bed that first night. He'd cry and I'd pick him up. This probably happened five times. He only had one accident. I decided not to mention that to Reba.

The dog was hiding under the kitchen table. I put out his food, but he didn't touch it. I put the bunny toy from Pet Universe next to him.

"You want to chew on this bunny?"

Shush sighed.

"Unlike other bunnies, this one won't mind."

Shush closed his eyes.

Reba was making oatmeal. I went to the refrigerator. "We're out of milk."

"I know."

"We're out of brown sugar."

She knew that, too. "We'll slice up a banana. It will

be healthy." She threw back her shoulders like she does when she needs to be tough. "And we'll be grateful."

It was healthy, but it wasn't that good. We hadn't talked about the mess we were in lately.

"So what are we going to do about that bank man and everything?"

Reba said she didn't know and walked outside.

"Look," I whispered to Shush, "you'd better eat what's put in front of you and be grateful because you could be in the pound right now."

Shush looked at the food and shuddered.

"It might be hard around here this month because we've got some big problems, but you know all about problems, don't you?" I scratched his head. He seemed to like that. "We're going to need to get used to each other. One thing you should know—you can count on me. I'm not one of those kids who says they'll do something and then forget."

I scratched his little head some more and made the bunny toy squeak.

"That's a good noise, right? Do me a favor—when you get around to chewing on this, pretend it's the bank man."

"What a lovely thought," Reba said from the porch.

Dear Mr. Jim,

I want to thank you for your generosity in giving me that bag of puppy food. I know my dog will love it when he gets over being so stressed. He's really chewing the life out of the bunny toy, though, and both my mother and I want to thank you for it. Last night my mother stomped on the bunny and it brought a smile to her face.

I've already mentioned your kindness to our neighbor and she said you'd never given her anything free and she felt the time had come. So if Mrs. Mulch comes over looking for free cat food, I know you'll know what to do.

Thanks again for being a friend to a lonely dog. If I meet any other needy dogs, believe me, I'll send them to Pet Universe.

Yours very truly,

Sugar Mae Cole

I'd just gotten back from mailing the letter. Shush was hiding under the kitchen table, but his food bowl was empty.

"Good boy! You ate. Now look, I'm here to protect you from whatever you're afraid of, but since that's, basically, the world, we're going to have to start small. Okay?"

Shush curled up in a ball.

"You know what? You're missing a lot of good things when you curl up like that. I want to show you something." I pointed to a picture on the wall of Mr. Leeland and Reba getting married. "See, these are my parents and neither one of them is doing too great right now." Shush sniffed the picture. "But despite that, I need to be brave, so I'm telling you this is possible. Do you know what Mr. Leeland did once? He told Reba he was going out to get gas for the car and he didn't come back for a month. That's like getting kicked, so we both know a little of what you went through." I petted Shush's head slowly to get him used to it. "I'm going to try to protect you from bad things, but I can't always be with you."

I gave him a treat, then he put his head in my hand.

"That's right. We love each other. Loving is good." I gave him another treat. "I wish somebody would try to train me with treats—chocolate would work." I got out a bag of M&Ms. He put a paw on my arm. "That's good. That's excellent. We're trusting each other. I think we deserve a treat, although chocolate isn't for dogs." I gave a dog treat to Shush and an M&M to me. "Okay, now,

I'm going to try something major." Slowly, I reached out my hand and gently stroked his stomach where he hurt. "I know you got kicked there, but I want to make it better." I petted him and then he backed off. "That's okay. We had a good time, right?"

And for the first time, Shush climbed in my lap and went to sleep. I gave myself an M&M for that.

Reba walked in holding a letter from Bergen and Bergen, Attorneys at Law, bad news written across her face. "They want us out by next Friday."

My mouth felt dry. "Can they do that?"

"I've called Mr. Leeland, and he said he would be coming presently."

Talk about double trouble. "You think that's a good idea?"

"I don't have any other ideas." She headed to her room.

I did.

I took a huge breath and made the hardest phone call of my young life. On the fourth ring, a lady answered.

"Grace Place."

I could hardly say it. "Is this where you come if you lose your house?"

"This is a place you can come," she assured me.

"I can bring my mom?"

"Yes. You and your mother are welcome."

I looked at Shush, who was mauling the bunny. I wasn't going to mention a dog just yet.

"So, if we need to do this, I just call back?"

"Where are you?" the lady asked.

"I'm at my house."

"All right," she said. "Let me get some information."

7

THE MONSTER WAS rising up.

"Yes, this is Reba Cole calling. . . . Yes, I did receive the notice. . . . Yes . . . but as I informed your office, Mr. Leeland, my husband, was unable to escort me to the courthouse. . . . I beg your pardon? I most certainly am not kidding. You see, this all has an explanation. . . . We can't possibly be out in seven days. . . ."

"Leeland, it's Reba. We're right up to the edge, darling."

If you asked me what I learned in school that week, I couldn't tell you. The only thing I remember was Mr. B taking me aside and saying I was a natural-born leader and he wanted to start developing all that potential in me.

I looked around and no one was lining up behind me. "I'm a leader?"

"It's pouring off of you."

I looked at my arms. I didn't see anything there

either, but Mr. B made me team leader for our language arts reading fair. My team was supposed to look at six books and decide why the authors wrote them.

"Because they needed the money," Peyton Crawler said.

I got home just in time for the worst day of my life.

There was a loud knock at the door. I jumped. Reba walked by me with her jaw set.

"Sheriff's office," a man shouted from outside.

Reba threw back her shoulders. "They most certainly cannot come in here. This is my father's house!"

"I know you're in there, Mrs. Cole!"

"Do not enter these premises!" Reba shouted. She was wearing her special GRITS shirt for the occasion. That stands for Girls Raised in the South.

It sounded like the door was being yanked off the hinges.

"Sheriff's office!" the man said again. "I've got an eviction notice for you, ma'am. We can do this the easy way or the hard way."

My bag was packed so full I had to use duct tape to close it.

"Go to your room, Miss Sugar," Reba directed.

I shook my head. "I'm staying right here."

She sighed. "All right then."

A pry bar broke the lock on our door and the sheriff busted in. He took one look at Reba standing there, small and pretty; she had all her makeup on and the sparkly earrings Mr. Leeland gave her the last time he won big at poker.

The sheriff coughed. "I hate this part of my job," he said.

Reba raised her chin and said each word slow. "I would dearly hope so, sir."

The sheriff gulped and looked at me. I glared at him with everything I had.

Reba stood there like a Southern belle who didn't take guff from anybody. "Mr. Leeland, my husband, has the check for the bank, but unfortunately, he has been delayed. I informed the bank of this. I informed your office."

Reba, if you think he's coming, you're crazy.

Reba raised her head like a queen. "I was told we'd have more time."

"I don't know who told you that, Mrs. Cole, but it's not true."

And two men began to carry our things onto the street.

Reba tried to get her cousin Guernsey on the phone, but there was no answer. She tried calling Mr. Leeland.

No answer anywhere.

I told her about the shelter, how the lady said we could go there.

"Certainly not," Reba said. "We can't leave our things on the street."

"What are we going to do, Reba? Where are we going to go?"

8

IT'S NOT FAIR, *but sometimes a kid has to act older than their age. You just pray hard to know what to do.*

I prayed and nothing came to me.

I needed to pee and didn't know what to do.

I rang Mrs. Mulch's bell, but she wasn't home.

I knocked on the Iversons' door—they weren't home either.

But I wasn't going to have an accident on the street, I'll tell you that; so I walked to our backyard, our ex-backyard, and stood behind a bush.

I remembered King Cole planting this bush when I was little.

I remembered his dog Murphy peeing on this bush.

Shush peed, then I squatted down, but not down enough, and got my underpants wet.

And that's when I started to cry.

x x x

I lay in the backseat of our car covered with a blanket. Shush was lying on the floor looking up at me. It was dark out.

I wondered if some criminals would come by and hurt us.

I wondered if the sheriff would come by and take us to jail.

I wondered how many monsters had surrounded our car already.

I was trying to think about other things so I wouldn't be so scared.

Like, you can live in a free country and not feel free at all.

You can try your hardest and it isn't enough.

I got born in the backseat of a Chevy, and here I was in another backseat trying to survive.

Dear Chevrolet,

How many people sleep in their cars, I wonder?

Do you think about that when you make the seats?

Don't tell me. I don't want to know.

"I can't do this, Reba. I need a place with walls."

"I know." Her voice sounded small. She reached over from the front seat and squeezed my hand.

I tried to pray like King Cole told me, but I couldn't. I felt like the earth had opened up and swallowed us into a dark place—a place no prayers ever got answered.

9

DEAR MRS. PITTMAN,

I want to thank you for hiring me a year ago and teaching me all your favorite old songs, especially "You'll Never Walk Alone." I've sung them for a few friends of mine, but they always have a crowd around them, so walking alone wasn't a big concern. I get it, though, and I'm trying, as the song says, to not be afraid of the dark.

I'm sorry I won't be able to work for you anymore—sorrier than you know. As I mentioned on the phone, my mom and I have to stay at our cousin's for a while and it's too far from your house for me to keep coming. I'm going to miss singing for you and feeding the ducks and talking to you about life. When I get really old, I want to be like you—full of life and trying new things, although bringing that baby duck into the house wasn't too great an idea with your cat and all. But nobody's perfect.

Thanks for giving me such a wonderful, crazy job.

I will always remember you.

Yours very truly,

Sugar Mae Cole

x x x

I was going to have to take two extra buses to get to school, because we were living outside the district at Guernsey's house. Reba said I couldn't tell anyone what happened either. I slapped this fake smile on my face.

I didn't know how to be at school now. I felt like I had a sign plastered on my head: HOMELESS GIRL. BEWARE. I lied to Meesha Moy, my best friend, and told her we had to stay with Guernsey's family because they needed our help. I lied to Woody when he asked why our house was locked up. I lied to Mr. B when he asked how I was. I felt like termites had gotten into my heart. I hated lying. I hated how good I was at it.

You know the definition of a loser? King Cole wrote. *Somebody who doesn't try.*

I was trying so hard.

"I know this girl," I told Mr. B. "She lost her house and it's been hard on her and her . . . father . . ." I coughed. "I was wondering . . . if you have any advice for this girl."

I waited.

Mr. B put his hands in his pockets and looked at me. His shirt read ACCEPT AMBIGUITY. We'd had *ambiguity* as a vocab word, but I'd gotten it wrong on the test. I could tell he was thinking about what I'd asked.

"Tell her I said that a house does not make a person—not by a long shot. It's what she's got inside that counts. Tell her that anyone who knows her well will want to help her. Tell her to not be afraid to talk to people that she trusts because there is help out there for her—more than she understands."

I looked down. "I'll tell her."

I don't know why, but the next day he handed me an envelope. "Give this to your friend. I did a little research. These numbers might actually be much higher, but this is what I found."

I went into the bathroom and opened it.

In case you were wondering if any famous people had ever been homeless, you're about to be amazed.

Two were nominated for the Nobel Prize—one of them won. Seven people won Oscars and five more were nominated for Oscars. Eight have won an Emmy, nine have won a Grammy, and that's not counting all the people who were also nominated for those awards. At least nine have been best-selling authors, and get this—one received the Presidential Medal of Freedom, and one person was actually knighted!

But let's not forget all the doctors, lawyers, nurses, teachers, scientists, artists, business people, and so many others who found their way out of homelessness to live remarkable lives.

I've got to tell you, I'm getting pretty inspired by this.

Mr. B

I didn't think girls could get knighted, but "Sugar Mae Cole, Nobel Prize winner," sounded pretty good.

I'm going to tattoo this across my heart!

Harper Wilhelm came into the bathroom, smirking at me. I think bullies take classes in smirking, because they all do it just the same. I didn't look at her.

"Sugar booger," she said.

I pictured Shush peeing on her ankle, and that felt good. Someday I'm writing a book and I'm going to name names.

x x x

Dear Mr. B,

You said the best leaders inspire people. I'd say that makes you the greatest leader in America. Thank you for what you gave me on homelessness. I think you should get the Presidential Medal of Freedom and your face should be on a stamp.

Yours very truly,

Sugar Mae Cole

x x x

"Well," Reba's cousin Guernsey kept saying, "I *guess* you could stay with us a little longer." He said it like we'd asked him to sell his soul to the devil and give us the money. "I don't know what much I can do," Guernsey kept telling Reba. "I've got two jobs and a family to feed." Guernsey liked Shush, though, so that was something.

Catching extra buses to get to school was tough, except for the lady who drove the second bus—she always had a good word for me. She'd say, "You go out there and set the world on fire."

"Yes, ma'am, I will." Every time she said it, I felt a little candle trying to light in my heart. It's hard to light a candle in the wind.

Reba and me did everything perfectly so Guernsey and his wife, Lou, wouldn't throw us out. We cleaned their whole house as often as we could, we made sweetie pies for them, and I taught Shush how to go to the door happy as anything the minute Guernsey walked in. That probably bought us a week or so.

"It's good to have family close by," Reba kept saying to Guernsey and Lou, but they would just look at her with flat stares.

One night I heard Guernsey and Lou talking in the kitchen.

"You tell them they have to leave now," Lou ordered. "I've had it. I want my house back."

"I don't know, Lou."

"Then I'll tell them."

I told Reba what was coming, but she said, "Nonsense. We're family."

Not that kind of family.

Finally Lou said, "We've loved having you—really. But we need our spare room back. I mean, there are shelters for people like you."

Not that long before, we'd been people like them.

Whenever you go through a fat mess of a time, try to learn something from it so you don't have to go through it again.

I've learned it's better to sleep in a car than with people who hate having you in their house and can't wait for you to leave.

I've learned about the power of a cute dog, too, even if he's nervous. People in houses think they need a dog. Believe me, no people on earth need a dog more than people in a shelter.

At least, that was going to be my big sales pitch when we got to Grace Place.

"They will not let you have a dog," Reba said.

I bent down and looked at Shush, who had curled into a ball, and I thought of King Cole settling into his big chair in front of the TV watching football, telling me, "The great Vince Lombardi always said, 'Winning is a habit. Unfortunately, so is losing.'"

Vince Lombardi was King Cole's favorite football

coach. He also said, "If it doesn't matter who wins or loses, then why do they keep score?" King Cole had these big truths framed on his wall. I wasn't sure the score was looking good for me and Reba. We lost our house, we got kicked out of Guernsey's place, and now we needed to stay in a shelter.

Three strikes and you're out. Of course, that's baseball. "In football," King Cole said, "you win by the inch. An inch in the right direction matters." He got this from a football movie.

Maybe I had an inch or so in me.

"You're a dog," I told Shush. "That's something to be proud of. I know what you've got inside. Go out there and do what you've got to do."

10

"YOU HADN'T MENTIONED a dog," the lady at the Grace Place desk said to me.

Reba shot me a look, but I said, "I know you help people get back on their feet, and Shush here has four feet, but they're little. He got kicked around a lot and I figured that's your specialty here."

I waited.

"I'll have to ask the supervisor."

That wasn't no. I followed her down the hall holding Shush in his blanket, because a picture is worth a hundred words. She could talk to her supervisor about some random brown and white dog, but when you look in Shush's eyes, you see he's got it where it counts.

She went into an office and shut the door. I waited for a while, then I knocked.

"Yes?"

"In case you want to see the puppy, he's right here." I put Shush down and patted him. "You'd better be ready," I told him. "You only get one chance. You've got to find it in yourself. Nobody else can do it for you."

The door opened, Shush sat like a good boy, and he looked up at her with his big black eyes.

"How cute!" she said.

Good start.

Shush wagged his tail extra adorably. She picked him up and he licked her chin. After a minute of that, she couldn't say no. I mentioned the call on his life to be a helper dog.

"Is he housebroken?"

"Yes, ma'am. He'll poop just about any place I tell him."

At the word *poop* Shush squatted down. I shook my head. "No, not here."

He stood up, waiting.

"That's remarkable," the supervisor said.

"Training dogs is a natural gift I have."

X X X

A long, thin room.

Two mattresses on the floor. Bathroom down the hall.

A skinny window that overlooked a noisy street.

Shush didn't like the noise much. "You'll have to deal with it," I told him. "You've dealt with harder things than this."

I laid our shoes against the wall as Reba whispered, "I'm so sorry, Sugar. My God, I'm so sorry."

Shush came over and climbed into her lap. Reba buried her face in his soft fur. "We won't be here forever," she said.

It just felt like forever. And close to the worst part was, I couldn't be in Mr. B's class anymore. This shelter was too far away.

"I'm sorry," Reba kept saying.

Sorry didn't cover it.

You keep saying that you're sorry,
But I wonder if you are.
I don't see you changing to make things better.
I don't see you reaching out to help me
Or getting any help for yourself.
Who's the mother anyway?
Is it you or me?

When I finished writing that, I cried.

I wished I had a rubber chicken to throw against the wall.

I wished I had someone in my life who knew about life.

Shush climbed into my lap and purred.

"Dogs bark," I mentioned. He kept purring.

My whole life was ruined because my mother couldn't say no to Mr. Leeland's gambling ways.

King Cole, if you're watching me up in heaven and you've got some advice, I promise I'll pay attention. I sat there with Shush waiting, but I didn't hear anything or feel anything or think anything.

Reba came into the room, climbed onto her mattress, pulled the sheet over her, and mumbled, "Nighty night."

Right.

I bent my face toward Shush's little head. "It's you and me, boy. We're going to have to act a whole lot older than we are. It would help if you could act more like a dog."

X X X

Reba's face was gray, her eyes were flat, and she didn't eat anything the next morning, my last day in Mr. B's class. I got to school late because none of the buses came on time. Reba came to sign me out of the school. I made a point of finding Meesha, who cried when I told her. Woody just looked down mostly and mumbled good luck. Marna was out sick, so I didn't get to say good-bye to her.

I sat through English and didn't say anything. I waited by Mr. Bennett's desk as the kids filed out. I looked at Claus the rubber chicken. This might be the last rubber chicken I ever saw.

"I can't come to this school anymore, Mr. B. Me and my mom, we're moving."

He leaned against the wall. "Where are you going?"

"We have to live with . . . friends for a while."

"Boy, Sugar, this is fast."

"It's been building." I handed him a blue envelope. "So I just wanted you to . . ." I started to cry. I was out of words.

"Listen to me, Sugar, you'll be fine wherever you go. You're an exceptional girl."

Not anymore I'm not.

"Look, do you want to talk to the school psychologist, because—"

I shook my head.

"Now, listen. You've got my e-mail and it's important that we stay in touch."

I gave him a hug and walked away from the best man in America.

Dear Mr. B,

You told me to write about the locked drawer, so here it is.

A key isn't just to open something,
It's to lock things up good and tight.
And when you lose a key, it's a big deal
because you can't get in or out.
That's what happened to my father.
He has a drawer in him with good things,
But it's locked tight and he can't find the key.
None of the keys I have will work.
This drawer has been locked up tight for years.
I wonder what's in there.
Has it gone stale like an old sandwich in a lunch box?
Does it have holes like old underwear?

Or is it new and waiting to be discovered?
I hope that's it.
I hope he has a better life to live and new things
to help him.
Sometimes I hate him, but mostly I just hurt.
I pretend like I don't care, but I do.
Maybe I have a locked drawer, too.

I will always remember you, Mr. B. Everything you taught me is written across my heart. I hope you feel good about that.

Yours very truly,

Sugar Mae Cole

11

THERE ARE LOTS of rules to follow in a shelter. You can't drink liquor, for one, but Reba breaks that rule sometimes. Normally she doesn't drink, except when Mr. Leeland is around, but she and this lady Evie, who lives at the shelter, they have a drink now and then in Evie's room. Reba snores in her sleep when she drinks. It's noisy enough here as it is.

It's good Reba and Evie are friends. They talk about everything together. My best friend at the shelter is Maxwell, one of the volunteers. He taught me how to make an omelette. He'd been a cook once in a restaurant, but now he works in a factory making cans. All day long, Maxwell makes cans. He says without cans the world would be a messy place because where would all that food go? He says cans are one of those things people don't think about, but they're everywhere in life, just like homeless people.

His dog Sparkle is with him tonight. Sparkle and Shush are friends. Maxwell taught me how to get Shush to come and lie down. He says I am a natural dog person.

He is showing me how to flip an omelette, which I am not so natural at. I flip it and miss the pan and it goes splat on the floor. Sparkle heads over to eat it.

Maxwell shouts, "Sit!" and this dog does just that, even though he's got fresh food right in his face. That's obedience.

I'm not too natural at that either, but I try to obey when it makes sense.

I obey at school for as long as I'm there, although I'm not doing so well in my new school. I miss Mr. B bad; I miss Meesha and Woody. Mrs. Mariah, my new English teacher, writes adjectives on the board. I've decided to collect adjectives, because they don't cost anything and they don't take up any room in my pack.

Glowing. That's my favorite new word.

The moon can be glowing. A person can be glowing.

The glowing girl giggled in the garden.

I would like to be that girl.

I wrote this poem about our garden.

Before we lost our house, we had a garden.
With lilies of the valley across the side of the house.
I can almost smell the perfume those flowers gave off.
Almost, but not quite.
We had peonies, too;
Bright pink ones that were so huge it didn't seem like they could be real.
The ants crawled all over them.
But the sunflowers were the best.
Sunflowers shoot up higher than any other flower because they've got attitude.
I wonder if the bank man is watering our flowers.
I wonder if people go by our house shaking their heads.
Someday I'd like to go back to that house.
Someday I'd like to go back to my old school.
This new school I've got, I don't like it or the kids.
I feel I've got a sign across my forehead that everyone sees:

HOMELESS GIRL.

Maybe it's just that I don't like me.

I didn't show that poem to anyone, but I did write the best paragraph in English about what animal we thought we were most like. I said a camel because I try to stop where I can and get a good supply of fresh water before my journey. I try to soak up whatever is good around me. I thought about sending it to Mr. B, but I didn't. I don't know why I haven't written him.

At school I hear kids say, "I'm going home."

"Come over to my house."

"When you get home . . ."

It's the most normal thing in the world, except when it's not.

When I get home
Someday.
I'll find my home
Someday.

I think a lot about someday.

Today some group brings boxes of canned goods

to the shelter. Teenage boys carry the boxes into the kitchen. I want to tell them, you did a good thing, but I'm too embarrassed. Once we collected cans of soup in Mr. B's class. Funny, I always thought homeless people were somebody else.

King Cole always said, you can't know someone until you've walked in their shoes. Somebody else said that before him, but he liked it so much he wrote it down in his autobiography. The thing people don't know, until they've been there themselves, is how tiring it is to be homeless. It's always heavy on you, like wearing a winter coat in summer. It makes you look down when you walk. You've got to work hard at looking up.

Reba's got the give-up look most days.

I'll do anything not to catch that. It can move like the flu through a shelter and get people sick. You hear them say: I *can't get no work. There's no work out there. I been done wrong by the world. I'm sick of being here and sick of listening to the traffic at night and sick of you looking in my face like I'm some kind of case.*

Get out of my space, you hear that?

You'd better get and not look back. But the ones I like say, *I'm going to get me a house someday. I'm going to take back what I lost*, and I tell them, *Yeah, you'll do it.*

That's the thing that's holding them up.

Reba's got a headache most days, so Shush spends time making sure she feels loved. Shush makes the rounds in the shelter, too. He makes Evie laugh when he purrs. Evie's got a loud laugh that wakes people up. He makes Marianne so hopeful she takes out a pencil and paper and draws the most amazing picture of him.

"That's wonderful, Marianne!" She's got his big eyes just right.

She shakes her head. "It's nothing special."

"It's close to the most special thing I've seen in a long time. How come you don't draw more?"

"I have a degree," she begins. Then she looks down. "You know, life isn't fair."

Maxwell has a vet friend, Dr. Dave, who gave Shush his shots for free. When he took me over there, it wasn't Dr. Dave's best day. I took that into consideration when I wrote my thank-you note.

Dear Dr. Dave,

Thank you so much for examining my dog Shush for free. You could have said no, since you'd just been puked on by a cat. I didn't think a cat could have that much in her stomach, but

I guess being a vet you're used to all kinds of animal barf. It's okay that you said that bad word in front of me. Believe me, I've heard worse.

My mother says that a good turn always deserves another, so I hope something great happens to you today.

Thank you for being a friend in need even on a bad day.

Yours very truly,

Sugar Mae Cole

x x x

Fall blends into winter, winter melts into spring.

Reba has some house-cleaning jobs, but not enough for us to get on our feet. She's been lonely, too, since Evie left with her baby a few months ago and moved to Illinois. She and Reba used to e-mail each other, but I think that stopped.

I know what it's like to miss people. I'd even listen to bad accordion music if I could walk home with Meesha again. I give Reba a head massage every night before bed to help her with her headaches. She closes her eyes and an almost peaceful look comes over her face. "You're a good girl," she says. "Sleep sweet, Miss Sugar."

"Feel better, Miss Reba."

At least she's not talking about Mr. Leeland showing up. I suppose that's something.

I try to help Reba remember who she is. "My mom is a great cook," I tell the church ladies who come on Wednesday nights with dinner.

The lead lady smiles and puts out a big tray of salad. "Is she now?"

"She makes these sweetie pies with buttery crust and pecan filling." I say it loud so the others can hear.

Reba looks down, but she's smiling a little. She's not talking much these days.

"She makes Southern soup, too, and maple corn bread."

The lady's half listening. "My, that sounds delicious."

It's lasagna night, and the church ladies brought a cake with thick white frosting. I ask for a corner piece of cake and hand it to Reba, who eats dessert first whenever possible. She looks at it confused.

"Extra frosting," I tell her. She nods a little, but doesn't eat it.

"And what would you like, honey?" the lead lady asks me.

I've told her my name the last three times she was here. "My name's Sugar," I remind her. "Sugar Mae Cole."

"Of course, of course. Such a sweet name."

There are forty-seven of us to feed tonight and we've all got names. I try to be good at names. When you have to line up to get things, it's nice to remember the people around you.

Lining up is a big part of life in a shelter.

So is holding it.

There's a line at the bathroom and I've got to go.

It kills Reba to have to line up. Sometimes she stands in line with her eyes shut like she's closing out the world. I let her go to the bathroom in front of me.

A lady, Billie, is laughing about how she scared a cockroach so bad it ran back into the wall. Marianne picks Shush up and holds him like a stuffed toy.

"I had a dog," Marianne says softly.

"Did you ever draw a picture of him?"

"No," she snaps. She's rubbing Shush in his sweet spot under his chin, his eyes are closed, and he's purring. The ladies are laughing at a purring dog.

Reba mutters something about "finding Sweet Street" on her way to the bathroom. Sweet Street isn't a real place, it's a place Reba believes is out there somewhere—a place without problems, a place with everything good.

I don't know about that, but the place I head for after the toilet is the shower. I turn on the water, throw my head back, and let the tears come. I recommend crying in the shower because you can get two things done at once.

Reba is quiet tonight, sitting on her mattress.

"Are you okay?"

"What?"

"Are you okay?"

She turns out the light and goes to sleep. Me, I toss and turn. Shush puts his paw on my arm.

"It's okay," I whisper to him. I'm not sure it is, but saying it feels good.

Later that night, I hear Reba sitting up in bed. The room's dark. "Reba?"

She sighs.

"I know I keep asking, but are you all right?"

"We're not making it here, miss." Her voice sounds far away. "I need to go someplace where the work is steady and there's insurance."

My mouth feels dry. "Like where?"

"Chicago."

"Chicago!"

She turns on the light. "There's a new cleaning

company there that really takes care of their people, and I can get a good job with benefits. Evie wrote me about it. She said we could stay with her and the baby until we find a place. We can start over."

It's not like I love the shelter, and I'm not sure this is a good idea, but my mother, she can clean houses, let me tell you. It's a natural gift she has.

"You know, Miss Sugar, I can clean up anybody's mess except my own."

Unfortunately, that's true.

12

THIS PLACE I'M at, it's got gargoyles on the roof. Big ones that you don't want to mess with. It's like they're saying, don't push it. Don't break the rules.

I've got to, though.

The computer I'm sitting at is on a table. The kids around me are on computers, too. I type in my e-mail address, homewardbound12@hotmail.com, and write,

Dear Mr. Bennett,

It's me, Sugar. I'm sorry I didn't write you back when you told me to, but I've been pretty busy with surviving and all. Right now I'm in Chicago to start a whole new life, which can be good or bad, depending. I just wanted you to know that being in your class was close to the best time of my life. I don't think teachers get a lot of thanks, so I wanted you to know I'm grateful.

Please write me back. It would be great to hear from you.

Yours very truly,

Sugar Mae Cole

I press SEND.

There's a whining sound at my feet. I make a whining sound, too. A man is helping a kid at a computer, a father, probably. He looks at me like I'm strange.

Mister, you don't know the half of it.

Now my green bag on the floor is squirming. I put my hands over it. There's another whine. I make a whiny sound, too.

"Are you all right?" the man asks.

I clear my throat.

"Your bag is moving," he mentions. He and the kid look at it.

"What's in there?" he demands.

"Mister, I'm just trying to use this computer. I'll be out of here in five minutes."

"What have you got in there?" he shouts.

I smile. "Just a poltergeist."

Now more people are looking at me and my wiggling bag, and this man won't let it be. He grabs the bag and Shush jumps out.

"It's a dog!" the kid shouts.

"Just a little one."

Shush lifts his leg and pees on the man's shoe—he deserves it, in my opinion. The father says a bad word as Shush leaps over a pile of books and tears past the librarian's desk.

Did I mention I was in the Chicago Public Library?

It takes a lot to get a librarian worked up. This lady shoves her glasses on her head.

"Was that a dog?"

"Yes, ma'am, but just a little one."

Now I'm hearing the voices of the other people as Shush runs free. Some are laughing. Some are shocked. The man-who-got-peed-on is telling the whole world what happened.

You should have let him be, mister. He was doing fine in the bag.

I run down a big aisle of books shouting for Shush, but I don't see him. Kids are running around looking for him.

"Shush!" I yell. It sounds kind of funny when you shout it.

"Is that your dog's name?" It's the librarian.

"Yes, ma'am."

"Why did you bring a dog into the library?"

This is a fair question. "Because he didn't have any place else to go."

Me either. I don't tell her that part.

I see a tiny brown tail wagging behind a copy machine.

"Good boy, Shush." A girl about my age scoops Shush up and gives him a hug. He puts his little paw on her shoulder and shudders. This is one of Shush's premier moves.

"Are you a little book dog?" she asks, laughing. Shush wags his stump of a tail.

If you need to sneak a dog into a library, make sure it's a cute dog.

"You have to take the dog out *now*," the librarian tells me.

I take Shush from the girl and go back and get my green book bag and my duffel. I put my bag on the floor, hold it open, make a *click click* sound, and Shush crawls right in.

"Will you look at that," someone says.

Training dogs is a natural gift I have.

"I'll take you downstairs." The librarian says it like an order.

The man-who-got-peed-on walks by glaring at me. I can tell he's about to say something not too nice, but Reba always says a kind word turns away anger.

I smile at him. "I think my dog likes you, mister. He wouldn't have done that if he didn't like you."

I try to make friends wherever I go.

I just got to Chicago.

13

I STEP OUT into the roar and rush of Chicago. Trucks crash by on Congress Street, cars zoom past. This city has a beat. Everything feels in motion. Shush shakes in the green bag.

"It's okay, boy. This is the biggest place we've ever been, huh?"

Tall buildings push to the sky. I walk tough like I've got places to go and people to see.

I'm really good at faking it.

I walk past the Panera restaurant that's not on my food budget, past a sign on a store that reads, STOP AND THINK.

Then, WHAT YOU'RE DOING.

The next sign, HOW YOU CAN MAKE A DIFFERENCE.

I'll have to think about that later; right now I'm trying to hold myself together. I walk next to a fancy building, through a covered walkway with big ceiling lights.

I'm not sure Chicago has a king, but if they do, he might like to hang out here. I look in the window of a little restaurant. There are apples on the counter. I could use an apple right now.

I pat the green bag. "Behave yourself." I walk inside.

I'm studying the apples. The guy behind the counter is watching me. I point to a little red apple that has a bruise mark. "You're probably not going to sell that one," I tell him.

He doesn't look too happy I mentioned that, but I'm not done.

I point at a slightly bigger apple with a gash in it. "I don't think you're going to sell that one either. Tell you what. I'll give you twenty-five cents for those two apples. I'd say that's a deal."

I hold out a quarter. He shakes his head. That's when Shush moves in my bag.

"Whatchu got in there?" the guy asks.

"My little brother."

The guy steps back. Shush moves again.

"It would mean the world to him to have an apple." I hold out a quarter and say into the green bag. "It's okay. He's a nice man. Don't do anything . . . you know?"

"Take 'em," the guys says fast.

I give the man the money, grab the two apples, and head out to the street. I hear a loud cranking, shrieking sound, like metal against metal, look up, and see a train going past high above the street. I wonder where it's headed. I'm thinking about what Reba said when we got off Big Bob's Budget Bus earlier today. "Right here, right now, Miss Sugar, things are going to turn around for us. We'll be on Sweet Street before you know it."

You should have seen her marching off today in her new shirt from the Salvation Army. She'd fixed the big rip in her flowered skirt with clear nail polish. Reba says just about anything can be fixed with clear nail polish, except a man.

A homeless man sits on the sidewalk with a sign, HUNGRY. People pass by, ignoring him. I nod at the guy and he nods back. I can't give him money, but I hand him my extra granola bar.

"I hope things turn around for you, mister."

He says, "God bless you."

Yeah, I'll take that. What people don't usually think about is this guy had a life before this happened to him. He had a before, like me.

I wrote a poem about my before. I was going to send it to Mr. Bennett, but I never did.

Before all this happened
I wasn't brave like I am now.
I didn't know I could take care of my mother
Or pee by the side of the road
and not get my underpants wet.
I didn't know that there's family that will help
you
And family that won't.
I didn't know,
But I know now.
Before all this happened
I had a room that didn't change.
I had a grandpa who was alive.
I had keys on a chain.
I had cookies cooling on a counter.
I had a porch and neighbors and a butterfly
named Fanny
Who would fly away and come back to visit.
I had my place in the world.
That was before.
Before is no more.

14

I'M WAITING FOR Reba in a place called Millennium Park; she's late again. This is one big park, let me tell you. I don't think Chicago does anything small. The problem with this park is I don't see any dogs. A man in a brown uniform walks by checking things out. I pat my green bag and look down. Dr. Dave said being in this bag was a safe place for Shush. I always have it opened just a little. I wish I could be in a safe, snug place.

I'm standing by what looks like a giant mirrored kidney bean. I'm not kidding.

People are moving around it, taking pictures, looking at the mirrors that show the big buildings and the trees and the crowd. You can stand underneath this thing. I walk to the center of it and look up. It's like a giant kaleidoscope of people just waiting for some huge hand to shake it and change the pattern.

I see my face with all the other faces.

HOMELESS GIRL.

Everyone probably knows that.

I stretch back my neck to look. Is this the girl I am?

My hair is shoulder length and brown and needs cutting. My eyes are light blue. I'm wearing my favorite shirt. It reads GOT SUGAR? I've got freckles across my nose, like Reba. I sure look tired.

There are two blonde girls in beautiful clothes, laughing and jumping up, watching themselves in this crazy mirrored bean.

Glowing girls.

I look away, because I don't want to see myself now. I look at the green picnic tables with umbrellas. People are sitting there talking. I sit at one, too, put my green bag on my lap and the duffel on the ground.

Homeless people get real good at waiting.

I'm thinking I was smart to go to the bathroom at the library and get cleaned up. I carry soap and a toothbrush wherever I go.

A man in a brown uniform walks by and looks at me. Maybe I should move to another place. If they know I've got a dog in here there's going to be trouble.

You've got to know the rules of the places you're at.

There are places you can sit and places you can't.

Places you can stand and places where they tell you to get a move on.

I taught myself to sleep in real noisy places.

I taught myself to sit and rest with my eyes open.

If you've got a place to live and money in the bank, you can sit anywhere. If you're homeless, it's called loitering.

x x x

I'm looking up at a huge wall that's got water coming down it. A man's face is on the wall, I don't know how many feet high. Mr. B. said there's no telling what a mind can create when it's having fun. Whoever thought this up was definitely having fun. I walk around it and there's another wall just like it. Between the walls of water and faces, there's a pond with kids jumping in the water; people are laughing and taking pictures.)

I'm too busy surviving to play.

I find a bench away from the crowd, put the green bag on my lap, put my face in the bag, and say, "Hey, it's me."

Shush wiggles a little.

"This is a non-dog park, so we have to be careful."

I reach my hands in the bag and give him my special

peace massage, which consists of me rubbing the curly brown fur around his neck and moving slowly down his back to his tummy. I created this massage myself. Shush purrs.

A bus screeches to a stop on the street and Shush starts shaking. "Good boy. That noise you heard? That was a bus. You've heard them before. We got here on a bus, so you're already on top of that." He looks up at me with his big eyes and twitches his little black nose. "Time for trust training. Even if you were kicked around when you were little, it doesn't mean that everyone is like that." I stroke him under the chin, which he loves. "Okay?"

Shush closes his eyes, which means yes.

"Good. And you've got to know that you can count on me one hundred and fifty percent." I rub him around his neck and he settles down a little. "That's good. And now I want you to know that even though you were a pre-owned dog, you were always supposed to be with me and Reba. The girl, Jenny, who first had you, she loved you, but not as much as me. I was getting ready for you and I didn't even know it. How cool is that?"

Shush wiggles in the bag, I can feel his little stub of a tail wagging. That's how he says, *Pretty cool.*

"And when we get a house," I whisper, "and I'm talking a good house now, with a yard for you and a room for me, and it will have blue walls and a kitchen where I can make an omelette. It's going to have a cookie jar, too, and your dog treats will be in a bowl by the back porch—all the normal stuff. But when we get there, we're going to remember these times when it wasn't so great, because like King Cole said, when you go through hard times you might as well pay attention and learn something."

A man on another bench is writing on his laptop. I bet he takes that thing for granted. Only once did I ask someone if I could borrow their laptop just for a minute to get Mr. Bennett's e-mail. The woman I asked said, "Get away from me. Who do you think you are?"

"I'm Sugar Mae Cole," I told her. "That's who I am."

I take out my folder that's got some of my writing. I'd like to send this poem to Mr. Bennett.

Here's what I wrote about being homeless.

I'm in front of you, but you don't see me.
I'm behind you and you don't much notice or
hear my voice.

If my dreams were shouts you'd probably call the police saying, some girl is screaming on the street and I can't sleep.
Make her stop.
But I wouldn't dare shout out my dreams because they're too young to be out on their own.
So I write some of them down and the others I carry in my heart.
I can tell you the places I've stayed, but that doesn't mean I've lived there.
I can tell you the people I've talked to, but that doesn't mean I knew them.
I can tell you something that all homeless shelters have in common—they've got people inside them that are holding on to their dreams as tight as they can, but feeling like they can't hold on forever.

I give Shush a biscuit. A man at a pet store gave them to me for free. Of course, I had to ask him if he would make a donation to the Cutest Dog in America Fund.

Reba's now two hours and fifteen minutes late. I hope she's not going for the record.

People walk by talking on their phones, staying connected.

I wish I had a phone.

I wish I was in a cozy kitchen eating warm cookies, surrounded by people who thought I was something.

I wish I was just starting sixth grade so I could go back to Mr. Bennett's class.

But I'm twelve years old, sitting on a bench in Chicago, waiting for my mother, and hoping like crazy she shows up.

15

I'M LUGGING TWO bags and walking Shush on Michigan Avenue, which isn't easy, but I find a place for him to pee. A huge truck rumbles by; Shush freezes in fear. He looks at me like, *Is any place safe in this world?*

I don't know if it's safe here, but when you've got to go you've got to go. "It's okay," I tell him. He does his business. I pick him up and cuddle him gently. "It's going to be okay," I say again.

I wish somebody would say that to me.

He won't drink the water I have for him. He's looking at the green bag.

"You want to go back in?" I make the *click click* sound and he crawls inside. I hoist the bag over my shoulder and walk back to the park.

"Meet me by the two crazy fountains with the faces,"

Reba had said, and she drew me a map. She was here two years ago with Mr. Leeland when they remarried after getting divorced. She kicked him out two months later when his gambling debts went through the roof. She still loves him bad, though.

"I keep seeing him changed," she told me. "I know there's a fine gentleman inside that man."

I'm trying to picture Shush as a mighty guard dog helping the helpless, but that's as big a reach as Mr. Leeland being a fine gentleman. I sit away from the crowd, eat the apple with the bruise mark, and save the bigger apple for Reba. I'm trying not to drink water so I won't have to pee, but it's hot and sticky. Not like Missouri, but still. I pour water into a paper cup, take a sip.

It's seven at night, not dark yet because it's June.

The flowers in this Chicago park are everywhere. I'm hoping Chicago is going to be as good as Reba said it would be.

"Well, Miss Sugar."

I turn around and Reba's standing there, but not in a good way. Not in the way she walked out of the bus terminal today when she went to get that job. All her makeup was just so, and her hair pulled back and shiny.

Now her dark hair is mussed and she's got the give-up look on her face.

My heart starts racing. "What happened?"

She takes her pack off her back like it weighs a thousand pounds, drops her other bag onto the bench, and sits down with a dead thump. "Nothing whatsoever."

My mouth feels dry. "What do you mean?"

Shush pokes his head out of the bag to greet her. She touches his head. "Nothing. No thing. There is no job." Her voice sounds far away.

That's not possible. We came all the way up here for this job.

"Did you see the lady?" I ask.

"I just told you."

"That's not telling me anything!"

Reba lowers her head, her hair falls over her face. "When Mr. Leeland comes . . ."

No! You're not going to do that here!

"Mr. Leeland," she says like a Southern belle, "will be coming directly for us—"

"He's not coming, Reba!"

Shush is looking at me. People walking by are looking, too.

"What about Evie? We're supposed to stay with Evie!"

She just sits there like she doesn't hear me.

"What about Evie, Reba? Where's her number?"

I grab her purse and look inside. A case with soap and a toothbrush, an old brush, mirror, tissues, underwear in a plastic bag. I find a printout of an e-mail. It's ripped and folded, and the date is January 14. It's from Evie to Reba.

> Hi Reba,
>
> How are U? I've found a good job with Maggie's Maids in Chicago—nice pay and everything. Maybe you could come and visit and get an interview. Let me know.
>
> Evie
>
> 312-555-6464

I stare at the e-mail. Today is June 3. "This is five months old, Reba!"

"Oh . . ."

"Did you tell her we were coming?"

Reba looks down.

"Did you tell her?" I scream. "And I mean recently? Did you call Evie when you got in?"

She looks at me, confused. "Her phone . . . it was disconnected."

I grab her arm. It has no strength in it. "Are you sure you called this number?"

She doesn't respond.

"What are we going to do, Reba? Where are we going to go?"

16

I'VE GOT TWENTY-NINE dollars in my pocket, a mother who's given up, and a dog who needs to pee.

I take Shush over to a street lamp on Michigan Avenue. It's dark now. I look down the wide street to a big bridge and tall white buildings with glowing lights.

A man across the street is playing a saxophone. His case is open for people to give him money. I feel like screaming.

Will someone please tell me what to do?

Reba is sitting on the bench rocking back and forth. A guy walks by, looking at her. He stops.

I don't like this. I scoop Shush up and run over.

He sits next to Reba on the bench. "Well, I've been watching you, honey . . ."

"Show's over!" I scream.

He turns his creepy smile on me. "You're pretty cute yourself."

"Get away from us! Get away!"

Shush is whining. The guy spits on the ground and puts his arm around my mother.

"Get away from her!"

"Mr. Leeland will be here presently . . ."

"Now, who's that, honey?"

I scream, "Help! Somebody, help!"

I keep screaming it until a man and a lady run over. The creep grumbles something and leaves.

Shush is shaking bad. Me, too.

"Are you all right?" the lady asks.

No. I take Reba's hand. "My mom, she's sick, I think. I don't know what's wrong."

The man tries to get Reba to talk, but she's hugging her duffel bag, shaking her head. . . .

"She's scared," I tell him.

He looks at Reba. "Ma'am, can you talk to me?"

I hold Shush tight. "She was supposed to get a job today. We were supposed to stay with Evie."

The lady takes out her phone. I hand her the e-mail with Evie's number. "Could you call this number, ma'am? This is who we're supposed to stay with."

The woman dials the number . . . waits . . . "It's disconnected. Let me try again to make sure." She punches numbers, listens, and shakes her head. "I'm sorry." She punches in more numbers, puts the phone to her ear.

Would somebody please tell me what to do!

17

A NURSE WALKS by in squeaky shoes; a phone rings. The policeman who brought us here talks with a man at the desk. We're in a hospital, the kind for emotions.

I've got the worst headache. I can't think. I press my hands against my forehead. "I need to see my mother, okay?"

A man in a white coat says, "You will. We have your mom upstairs and we're going to be talking with her to see how we can help. She'll need to be here for a few days."

He doesn't understand. Reba and me, we stay together. "I need to see her now."

"I'm afraid that can't happen for a little while."

"No, look, wherever her bed is, I can sleep on the floor, I've done that before."

He shakes his head. "We don't allow that here. I'm sorry."

He's not sorry.

He asks me questions.

Age?

Twelve going on twenty.

Address?

We don't have one yet.

Phone?

We don't have one of those either.

Nearest relative?

That's Reba.

In addition to her?

There's no more addition in my family. Me plus Reba equals two.

You have no one to call, Sugar?

All I have is Mr. Bennett's e-mail, not his phone.

I look down at the green bag. I'm sure not telling him about Shush.

A woman in a green striped shirt, black pants, and star earrings walks up.

"Sugar," the white coat man says, "this is Dana Wood. She works with children and family services. She'd like to talk to you."

Dana Wood looks at me and I look away.

"You want to tell me what happened tonight, Sugar?"

"I just told the other guy."

"We like to gather our own information. I can see how it might seem unnecessary."

I don't want to say it all again. I'm tired.

"Let's sit down over there and talk."

I stand up. I don't want to sit down and talk. "When can I see my mother?"

"Tomorrow, probably. We want you to be able to see her very soon. She's safe, and the staff here knows what they're doing."

I don't like the sound of this. "What do they do?"

"It will depend on what they find."

That's a non-answer. "What are they looking for?"

"Well, to begin with, they want to understand what kind of stress she's been under."

"You tell them she wasn't scared like this when we had a house. She was so much stronger then."

"I'll make sure they know that, and it would be good for you and me to talk about that some more, but it's late and you look tired. I think it would be best for you to stay someplace for a little while so your mom can get back on her feet. It's a group house and—"

"No!" I bolt away from her. That gets Shush moving around. I knew a kid from St. Louis who got beat up in a group house.

"What's in your bag?" she asks.

Be cute, be really cute.

I take off my pack and Shush climbs out.

Dana Wood is shocked. "You have a dog . . ."

"Just a little one." Shush wags his tail. "He's going to be a helper dog, okay? He's got to be in hospitals so he can practice."

Shush looks around at the bright lights and shudders. "He needs a lot of practice."

Dana Wood shakes her head. She puts out her hand toward Shush. He sniffs it. I'm studying this lady. She's got caring eyes, that much I can say. King Cole always said, *You want to see what a person's about? Look them in the eye.* So I do.

She's petting Shush's head. "Sugar, I doubt you can bring this dog to—"

"I have to bring him!"

Her phone rings. She snaps it open. ". . . I'm with someone right now. . . . No, I can't take on another . . . I understand that, but, I'm full up as it . . ." She listens awhile and sighs. "All right . . . I'll get there as soon as I can."

She looks at me. "My boss is out of town and I'm doing double duty. My colleague Bill Marston will take care of you. I have an emergency at the police station."

"I'm an emergency, too!"

X X X

I'm sitting at a desk at this hospital for emotions, using the computer to get my e-mail. I type in my address, homewardbound12@hotmail.com.

You've got to carry your dream around with you. You've got to make sure it's in your face so you won't forget.

The screen pops up. I've got mail from Mr. B!

Hello, Sugar.

I'm so glad to hear from you. I saw something today that made me think of you. It was a sign that read,

MOST PEOPLE DON'T UNDERSTAND HOW
IMPORTANT THEY ARE.
TELL SOMEONE YOU KNOW TODAY.

So I want to let you know how much I respect you, how much I believe in you, and how much you added to my class when you were here.

Let me know how you're doing. I believe in

you. I guess I already said it, but I want you to hear it double strength.

How is your writing coming?

Claus sends his best, as do I.

Mr. B

I picture him leaning against his scratched desk twirling the rubber chicken in the air. I feel like he's holding out his hand for me to take, so I grab hold of it.

I don't know how to tell him how I'm doing.

I type:

Mr. B,

You're the best! Keep writing to me, okay? I've written some poems on what's been happening to me. Would you like to read them?

Tell Claus I said he's a good chicken.

Sugar

I press SEND, then I press PRINT and a copy of his e-mail whizzes out of the copier. I fold it neat. I'm going to sleep with this under my pillow, if I get a pillow, that is.

I feel so tired.

I wonder if Reba's sleeping, or if she's lying there scared. Sometimes she can't sleep, especially if it's noisy. She and Shush are alike that way.

"I think this dog has to go to the bathroom!" Bill Marston lifts Shush up the way I do when it's okay to pee.

"That's not the way to—" I begin, but Shush thinks it's his signal and he lets loose. "I'm sorry."

The lady in the office starts laughing—easy for her, she steered clear of the spray.

18

AN OLDER BOY looks at Shush. "I had a dog—it died. It kept barking, so my uncle shot it."

A girl looks me up and down and says, "It's hard here for the first couple days."

Another girl laughs. "Then it gets harder."

The woman who runs this place, Janine, has a tired smile. I tell her how Shush has a call in life as a helper dog and she says, all right, he can stay here, but if there's any trouble . . .

"We won't be any trouble." Shush cocks his head.

This group house I'm at, it has a TV and two old couches. Kids older than me are watching a show about missing people and how the FBI looks for them.

Reba's missing.

I know right where she is, but she's missing just the same.

Janine with the tired smile shows me my room. It has a funny smell. I can hear the TV.

Castilla Farmer was last seen at the grocery store.

Mitchell Louden was last seen at the garage where he works.

Reba Cole was last seen, the way she used to be, at her home in Round Lake before the sheriff came to take it.

"There's no lock on this door," Janine mentions. "We've been meaning to fix it. You need anything?"

Just my old life back.

She pets Shush on the head and leaves. I shove a chair in front of the door, take out Mr. Bennett's e-mail, and read again about how I'm important and I probably don't know it.

"I'm important," I tell Shush. "You are, too." He presses into me.

A girl screams. I rush out holding Shush. Janine is shouting something. The girl is standing on the couch pointing, and the older boy is laughing.

A rat races across the floor, fat and ugly. Shush goes stiff in my arms.

The older boy shakes his head.

Shush is trying to get free.

"You want to get it?" I put him down. He runs toward the rat, who runs behind a radiator. I've never seen him like this, but I'm not telling them that.

Shush stands there waiting.

"I want to get me a dog," the older boy says. "Where'd you get that dog?"

"At Walgreens in the dog section," I tell him.

The group starts laughing. Janine says, "She got you, Ray."

"Maybe you'll give me that dog."

"You leave us alone!"

I grab Shush and go into my room, my heart pounding. I put the chair against the door. It's so hot in here.

"That thing you did with the rat was excellent."

Shush wags his little tail.

"If anybody tries to come in here, you do that again. Okay?"

I open my pack and take out King Cole's autobiography, *Upon These Truths I Stand.* I turn to chapter ten, "Keep Marching."

When you don't think you can keep going,
You might be right,
But just in case you're wrong,

Keep marching.
When you're flat out and don't know what to do,
It might be a while before you know,
But don't give up,
Keep marching.
If your feet are sore,
Keep going.
If you hear a roar,
Keep moving.
When the worst that can happen has come and gone
And you're still standing,
Remember that you won.

—O. Kingston Cole, written upon the occasion when a tornado hit Plainview, Georgia, and tore up my house, leaving me and my family homeless

They moved to Savannah after that and life began to turn around for them, that much I know. Reba doesn't talk about it much, except for how she worked for Miss Amanda Risserwell, her number one role model next to Mother Theresa.

Reba was always saying, "My goodness, the very first time Miss Amanda met me, she said, 'Reba Cole, you don't come from means and you don't come from heritage, but you've got the heart of a Southern belle nonetheless'—well, I near about fainted."

I never once thought that homelessness would visit my family again. It's like a tornado hitting twice in the same place. Isn't there a rule that's not supposed to happen?

I don't like the noises in this house. I jump at every one.

I put Mr. B's e-mail under the pillow.

I lie back on the bed and hold *Upon These Truths I Stand* over my heart.

I wonder if King Cole can see me from heaven.

I wonder if God is paying attention, or if he's off helping people who have places to live.

I take out the card Dana Wood gave me with her phone number and e-mail. I wonder if she'll forget that I'm here.

"We need to stay awake," I tell Shush. "It's a long time till morning."

"He bites," I say.

The guy starts laughing.

"In the middle of the night," I tell him, "he attacks with no warning. He doesn't look like he would." Shush starts shaking. "But he does."

"Why's he shaking?"

I gulp. "He's got this energy inside, it's so strong it makes him shake." The boy looks at Shush, not sure what to think. "He shakes before he bites."

The boy steps away. I go into the bathroom and call Dana Wood's number again. Her voice mail beeps. My head is pounding.

I need Dana Wood, not a beep.

"This is Sugar Mae Cole. I want to remind you where I am. Actually, I'm not sure where I am exactly, but it's not a good place for me. You've got better than this, right?" I close my eyes. "Here's what I want you to think about: if I was your daughter, where would you want me to be?"

I hang up, then I realize, if I was her daughter, I'd be living with her. I call back.

"That message I just left? What I meant to say is, if you were me, where would you want to stay? You've got to put me and Shush there right away. We're already packed. And I want to remind you that you said I could see my mother. That's got to happen soon, too, because she doesn't do well without me. I'm not kidding." I clear my throat. "Okay, so have a nice day."

I hate leaving life-and-death messages.

20

DEAR JANINE,

Thanks for giving me and my dog a place to sleep when we didn't have any place to go. If you'd said that Shush couldn't stay, I would have thrown an ugly fit, but that didn't have to happen. I can't say that being with you was the best thirty-six hours of my life, it was actually pretty bad, but I bet you're used to scared kids showing up and not knowing what to do. You've got a good selection of cereal, though, and the raisins weren't all that hard. I've seen worse.

I would suggest you get the locks on the doors fixed and you take care of the rat right away. About that boy who walks around without his shirt? Watch your back when he's around.

I hope you have a good life and that me and Shush weren't too much trouble.

Yours very truly,

Sugar Mae Cole

x x x

Two kind faces—a man, a woman.

"Well," the woman says, "we're happy to have you here. Your dog is so cute. He's a quiet little thing."

We walk up a staircase past peeling wallpaper and family pictures; the hall light is bright.

"You're right next to the bathroom."

I hope it locks. "Thank you."

"Here are some towels."

"Thank you."

"Would your dog like some water?"

"Thank you, ma'am."

"My name's Lexie, and this is my husband, Mac."

Dana Wood had to do some talking to get me here. I don't know why.

"Is there anything else you need?" Lexie asks.

I can't begin to answer that.

Lexie is fluffing the pillow in this pink room. I'm going to put Mr. Bennett's e-mail under that pillow. She says, "You look a little like our daughter when she was your age."

Whatever you say.

"We're right down the hall if you need anything."

I don't need much.

"That's the quietest dog I've ever seen."

"He has to be quiet or I couldn't keep him."

Lexie smiles. She's round and pretty; the top she's wearing has rainbow colors. She pauses at the door. "You've been through it, I know, honey. We're going to do everything we can to help you."

Shush is playing on the shaggy rug, rolling over on his back and wiggling. This is a pretty serious moment, so I try not to smile. Lexie laughs at Shush.

"I like a dog with spirit."

"He's got that."

This room I'm in, it has a white bed. I wonder what color Reba's room is at the hospital.

"Your mom is safe at that hospital," Lexie tells me. "They know what they're doing over there."

People keep saying that. "You take kids in all the time?"

"As often as we can." She's got a sad smile. "Try and get some sleep."

"Are there other kids here?"

"Just you. We only take one at a time."

"Can I take a shower first?"

"Of course." She hands me a cup that has a toothbrush and toothpaste in it.

I go to the bathroom and Shush trots after me. I let him come in.

"Sit." Shush sits on the green rug.

I lock the door, turn on the water, and take off my clothes. Shush grabs one of my socks and chews it as I step into the shower and feel the good, clean water run over me. I lather up the soap and wash myself again and again, getting the road dirt off. I wash my hair with shampoo that smells like apples. I take a long shower. Nobody is in line waiting for it, like at the shelter.

As the water pours over my head I start to cry. I pound my fist against the shower wall, but it's okay. No one can hear you when you're crying in the shower.

x x x

When I first wake up, I don't remember where I am. The sun beams through the window. Shush is awake, watching me. He walks over—cold nose, warm heart.

Now I remember.

I put out my hand. "You okay?"

Shush puts his head against my hand and hugs me. It's quiet in this house, not like the shelter. I lie here in this soft, warm bed. Out the window I see yellow flowers growing around a pole. This was their daughter's room, I bet. White dresser, pink quilt, silver mirror.

Mirror, mirror on the wall . . .

I look away from the mirror; people say I'm pretty, but I haven't felt pretty for a long time.

I want to see my mother.

Shush is sniffing the shag rug. "I'll be right back, boy." I open the door, head to the bathroom. He follows, whining a little.

"What is it?" He looks deep into my eyes—this dog understands everything. You can't ask for more than that in a pet.

I wash my face, and this time I look in the mirror and try to see a normal girl with happy eyes and a life that doesn't need changing, a girl who has a shiny key ring with keys to her own house. That's my dream.

"Did you sleep well?" Lexie says it from the other side of the door.

I guess they all ask this. "Yes."

"Good. Are you hungry?"

"Yes."

"Would you like pancakes?"

I grin at Shush, who cocks his head.

"With chocolate chips?" she adds.

I open the door a crack. "I didn't know they came that way."

She smiles widely. "Anything else, honey?"

"Sugar. My name's Sugar."

"Sorry. I call lots of people honey."

But about the anything else, yes there is. "I need to see Reba."

21

REBA SITS IN a chair by the window. She doesn't notice me standing by the door. She's wearing a robe and slippers and is humming a song I know too well, "Stand by Your Man." I look at Dana Wood, who brought me here. I don't know how to tell her this is a dangerous song.

I go over to where she's sitting. "Hi."

I wish they'd turn the stupid TV off.

Heather, I know that you killed Alonzo in cold blood. A TV actor says that.

You tracked him down, didn't you, Heather, after what he did to your sister.

She turns slowly to look at me, like she just woke up. "Hi." She reaches out and touches my hand, then her hand drops back into her lap. Her face looks sad and gray—give-up gray.

I gulp. "How are you?"

She looks down and sighs. "Tired."

"You can get some rest here."

She shakes her head.

I kneel down next to her and take her hand. "It's going to be okay." I look in her eyes and it's like some alien came, sucked my mother out, and left her core.

"I don't know what happened," Reba whispers.

I don't either.

"I did everything I knew how to do. You tell them."

"I will . . ."

She shakes her head. "You tell them."

Her dark brown hair is hanging over her face. I gently lift it back and say, "They don't know how hard it's been."

She puts her small hands over her face.

I don't know how to help you, Reba. I don't know what to say.

"Shush slept on a fuzzy rug last night. He's acting good. And me, I'm okay." I want to make sure she heard that. "I'm okay, Reba."

She nods and looks out the window. I look at Dana Wood, who gives me a smile. I talk about some things that don't matter, like how it's sunny outside, I'm sleeping in a pink room . . .

Reba smiles sad.

I stay with her a little longer and then the nurse comes in and says we have to go.

I give Reba a long hug. She tells me, "Stay sweet."

She's been saying that since I was small. I don't think it's right to leave, I should be sleeping on the floor in case she needs something. I think she needs a lot right now.

"I love you, Reba."

She puts her hand on my head, then goes back to looking out the window.

Dana Wood says she'll check in on her in a few days, and we follow a nurse down the hall.

I don't look in any of the rooms, I don't look at the nurses' station, I don't look at the doctor coming toward me, I just look to the door that I came through earlier, and now I realize it isn't an open door, it's locked. The nurse opens it with a key and out we walk, free. But I don't think Reba's free to leave here.

I'm not sure how to be with that. I feel scared, the kind of scared that makes you cold.

When we first lost our house, I told Reba, "I just want things to go back to normal. When is that going to happen?"

"Soon," she promised.

Soon seems awfully far away.

"Your mom's on medication that makes her tired," Dana Wood explains.

"What's wrong with her? She's never been like this." I'm trying to get a breath. I feel sick to my stomach all of a sudden.

"The early diagnosis is that she had something called a severe depressive incident. That can happen when people are very stressed and then something tough happens and they can't bounce back."

I sit down. "Like not getting the job she was counting on?"

"Exactly. It was the last straw, and she shut down."

"She made it bigger in her head than it really was."

"That happens often, Sugar."

"But it's not normal, right? Normal mothers don't do this!"

"What I can tell you is that most people sometime in their lives make something bigger in their heads than it really is."

"But they don't end up in the hospital!" I'm trying to breathe normally, but it's hard.

"Sugar, the doctors and nurses here know how to help."

That doesn't tell me anything. "How long does she have to be here?"

"A week, probably."

"Then what?"

"We're not sure yet, Sugar."

I'm getting tired of this. "I want to talk to somebody's who's sure."

"I'd feel the same way if I were you, but right now, no one's sure."

I have another question, but I'm not going to ask it.

Could this shutting-down thing happen to me?

x x x

I'm writing poems at night because I can't sleep.

How are you doing?
Everybody wants to know.
It's like there's a special answer they're looking
for.
Fine—I'm doing fine.
Or pretty good.
Or okay, I'm okay, you don't have to worry
about me.

They should probably worry, though, just a little,
Because I'm feeling like I could turn to stone
right now
So I would stop feeling.
The stone girl.
You can't get me.
You can't hurt me.
You can't make me go anywhere I don't want.
Girls don't wake up saying, I'm turning to stone
today.
Normal girls don't have to do it,
I'm not supposed to do it,
But stone is strong
And it's hard to break.
Not like a heart—that's easy to break
And hard to put back together.

Then I wrote this just before morning came.

My mother is in a locked place.
It's not just a door that locks,
It's in her mind and her heart.
I watched a little of the door shutting
But I didn't understand what was happening.

I hardly do now.
I hope she will remember all that's shut up with
her.
Her smile and her sweetness and her grit
and her courage.
She raised me alone mostly, except for King
Cole.
She worked and she cried
And she didn't give up until now.
But I'm not giving up on her
Because for all those years she didn't give up on
me.

22

DEAR MR. B,

Do you remember when you told us to write about what we know?

Well, here are two poems I worked hard on. I'm not looking for a grade or anything like that, I just want to know that you have them.

Yours very truly,

Sugar Mae Cole

An hour later, I get this back.

Dear Sugar,

Wow. These are so good, and it's not just because you wrote about what you've experienced. You opened your heart; the words came out honestly. I think, at a young age, you've learned not to be afraid of the things that hurt you. You're putting them out there, and that's power.

I'm sorry that you've had such a tough time, but you seem to be able to pull beauty out of it. All your courage shines through. I feel confident in saying this—no way are you going to stay where you're at.

Life is going to turn around for you.

Because these are so excellent, I've created an award, and it is my honor to bestow upon you the first Michael R. Bennett Prize for Being Exceedingly Courageous and Insightful in Middle School. This is close to winning the lottery, except there's no cash involved.

I do want to ask you—are you in a safe place right now with people you trust?

Write me back, Sugar Mae Cole. If you don't, Claus and I are going to be really irritated.

Mr. B

I write him back and tell him I am safe.

I sit at the computer reading Mr. B's e-mail again

and again, drinking in his words.

Here's what I wrote next, but I didn't send it.

We celebrate the wrong people sometimes.
We should wake up and see who the real heroes are and give them the star treatment.
I nominate Mr. Bennett for star-hood.
Here's how his life should go.
His pickup truck is surrounded by his adoring fans.
He waves, signs a few report cards, and drives off as the crowd screams.
Mr. Bennett makes Time magazine's list of Most Influential People.
Greatest teacher in America is awarded the Nobel Prize for Everything
As rubber chickens take the country by storm.

23

THE BOY AT the front door has curly dark hair. He is holding clippers and a trash bag. It's morning.

"Mac said I'm supposed to clear the front, but I'm not sure what he wants done with the stuff by the tree," he tells me.

"I don't know."

"Is he here?"

I don't know that either. Shush comes to the door wagging his tail. The boy says, "Hey there, puppy." And Shush jumps up on the door.

"You're new," the boy says to me.

"Yeah." I'm not giving more information than that.

"I work for Mac. I'm Dante."

"I'm Sugar and this is my dog Shush."

"Sugar and Shush." He says it like Dante isn't a weird name, too. Mac pulls up in his truck and waves. Now Shush is going crazy to get outside. I open the door and he jumps all over Dante, who laughs and turns around; Shush turns around, too. Dante starts running, Shush runs after him, then Dante stops and Shush does, too.

Mac walks up holding some pots of coral-colored flowers.

Lexie comes to the door. "Good color."

Mac puts the plants down and Shush runs over, sniffs them, and pees right on one of the planters.

"Well," Mac says, "I guess they're ours now."

He shows Dante what he wants done by the tree and Dante starts to work. I'm a good worker, too. Right now, I could use something to do.

"How are you with flowers?" Lexie asks me. I tell her about my champion sunflower in fifth grade.

"If you want to, you can help Dante plant those begonias in a ring around the tree. He'll show you what to do."

I head over and Dante says, "You understand that when you take a plant out of its starter box, it gets nervous."

I'd never heard it until this minute, but I don't want to seem stupid. "I know that," I tell him.

"So when you take the plant out, you've got to do it real gently. It's kind of shocked to be in a new place."

I know what that's like.

He puts the plant near the hole he's digging. "Now I've just got to dig it out a good new place where it can really grow. So I'm putting the mulch down in the hole, and this plant food, see?" He sprinkles something in the hole. "Now I'm putting some water in—just a little." He puts the plant in and covers it with dirt.

"Where are you from?" he asks me.

"Round Lake, Missouri."

"Is it really round?"

I laugh. "Not really."

"You have a family?" he asks me.

"A mom." I start digging a hole. I don't want to talk anymore.

"Where is she?"

I guess everyone knows this is a foster care place. "She's sick and has to be in the hospital."

He looks up at me. "Which hospital?"

I look down. "I forget the name." I watch him dig another hole and put the mulch in. I copy him just so. I'm always looking to see somebody do something well, so I can copy it. King Cole said you can learn a lot about how the world works by watching people do things right.

I take my plant out of its container, put it in the

hole, put fresh dirt over it, and pat it down.

"You're pretty good with flowers," Dante tells me.

It's a natural gift I have.

Shush runs over and sniffs the dirt. "Sit," I tell him. Shush sits right there.

"You're good with dogs, too." Shush wags his tail.

"How come you got named Dante?"

"My mother loves this writer named Dante." He laughs. "He wrote about hell and stuff."

"You got named after somebody who writes about hell?"

"He was a great man of his time. She wanted me to have a voice in the world." Dante plants another flower. "How come you got named Sugar?"

Sweetness is hard to explain. I dig another hole.

I look at the little plant in my hand. "It's okay," I whisper to it, and put it in the hole.

x x x

"Can you tell me a little about your mom, Sugar?"

Dana Wood sits back in an ugly brown chair and waits for me to answer.

Explaining Reba isn't the easiest thing.

"I can tell you that before we lost our house and she

got sick, she was pretty happy, except when Mr. Leeland came around. Being homeless just about killed her."

"What do you mean?"

If I could take Dana Wood back to our house on Pleasant Street, and she could see Reba sitting on the front porch in her white wicker chair smiling at the people who went by, she might understand.

"She wants the world to be nice," I say. "She wants it to be gentle."

Dana Wood writes that down.

"She used to write thank-you cards to everyone. People loved getting them."

I used to write them, too.

"I haven't gotten a thank-you card in a long time, Sugar."

I look out Dana Woods's window to the dirty building across the street. "She wants life to be sweet." I'm not explaining this too well. "Reba should have been born rich so she could sit out on her veranda and give people iced tea and sweetie pies and talk about things that aren't upsetting."

Dana Wood writes that down. "And when things get upsetting . . . what happens?"

I shift around.

I don't want to say the wrong thing, but I don't think lying is going to help anybody. "Sometimes she looks the other way."

"Can you remember a time when she did that?"

"When Mr. Leeland would come over drunk and ask to borrow money. She'd always make excuses for him."

More writing.

"But write this down, too. She can be strong. You should have seen her when the sheriff came to take our house."

I feel the sense of it hitting me all over again.

I close my eyes. *I don't want to talk about this anymore.*

x x x

I'm back in the pink room.

Tell me about your mother.

I wish I'd done a better job describing her. Reba's got all these parts, and you've just got to hang out with her to understand how they all fit together. That's the thing Mr. Leeland didn't get—he didn't want her to be her real self. He wanted her to be this helpless Southern lady who fluttered her hands and didn't think for herself.

I open my writing folder and take out the craziest

thank-you note ever. It's from the last time Reba and I played the thank-you note game. She's an ace at this game. She should be, she made it up. The point of the game is to write a thank-you note for an unbelievable situation.

I could see Reba taking a fresh thank-you card from the box she kept on our kitchen table. She said, "Situation, please," like she was on a TV game show.

I tried to sound like a game show host. "Aliens have landed and taken us captive in their spaceship, and after giving us a ride around the sun, they bring us back home."

Reba touched her southern bell necklace, thinking.

"It was a cool spaceship, too," I added. "You have two minutes to write the note . . ." I looked at my watch. "Beginning *now*."

Reba looked off into the distance to get an idea. She tapped her pen and started writing. I was dying to look over her shoulder, but that's against the rules.

"Sixty seconds," I told her.

She wrote faster.

"Thirty . . ."

"And the countdown. Ten, nine, eight, seven . . ."

She signed her name, underlined it just in time, and handed it to me.

Dear Creatures,

Thank you for the ride in your spaceship. It was very clean, and I must say, being with all of you and trying to focus on all the eyes you each have on your heads made me and my daughter see things in a new way. I'm sure that you all come from good homes on your planet, and I will be letting the rest of the earth know how kind you were to me, although perhaps you want to rethink hovering over my backyard and sucking me into your jet stream. It did take me a few minutes to stop screaming and get to know you. I'm not being critical, it's just a suggestion. The next time you're in the atmosphere, please stop by for tea and sweetie pies.

Yours very truly,

Reba Cole

"Reba Cole," I shouted, "you are our grand prize winner!"

She laughed. "What do I get?"

I wished I could give her the world.

I miss the old Reba.

24

THE 151 BUS pulls up, and Lexie and I get on. Big Bob's Budget Bus had a slight sour smell; this bus smells better. It heads down the street and I look out the window at the stores and the people walking by.

"Ladies and gentlemen," the driver shouts, "feast your eyes on this fine city. We're glad you're here."

That makes me grin, and I look at the big streets and the tall buildings and wonder if I should feel happy when Reba is locked up in a mental hospital. The thought of that makes me tired.

Lexie doesn't seem like she ever gets tired. She's pointing out buildings and a big park. "That's Lincoln Park," she tells me. "There's a zoo in there, boats on a pond." She points down a street. "Best ice cream in Chicago is that way. What's your favorite flavor?"

It's been so long since I got to choose, I just eat whatever people hand me. "Chocolate chip," I tell her.

"We need to get you some of that."

Reba's favorite is maple pecan—that's not easy to find, but back when we had our house, she'd buy vanilla ice cream, let it soften, put it in a bowl, and stir in some maple syrup and toasted pecans, then she'd freeze it again. We'd eat it in big yellow bowls on the porch. Those bowls got broken when the sheriff came and carried all our stuff to the street.

We used to cook up a storm in our kitchen—we'd make lovely pizzas, hamburger soup, and sweetie pies, the best dessert ever. They're like little pecan pies with buttery dough.

Today Lexie and I are heading to her favorite store to get me some clothes, not used ones, either. I look out the window at Chicago. I never want to leave this big, wonderful place.

I look up on the wall of the bus. There's a poster of a homeless man sleeping on the street and the words GET HIM THE HELP HE NEEDS.

I study the picture of the homeless man. It doesn't tell the story. In his heart, that man's got dreams he's packed away.

Lexie says, "Come on, it's our stop."

"You ladies have a good day now," the driver says.

Lots of people say that, but this guy says it like he means it.

I smile back at him, and the craziest feeling comes over me.

I almost feel normal.

Of course, my mother's in a mental hospital and just the other day I didn't have a place to sleep, but sometimes feelings are like a butterfly landing on your arm for a few moments. King Cole told me that.

"You just enjoy them while they're perched there," he said.

That man was an official genius.

The whole world should know, but they never will.

x x x

"What's your favorite color?" Lexie asks me.

"Yellow."

We're standing in a store that's got more clothes than I've ever seen. Lexie marches to a rack of tops and goes through them with total focus. She lifts up three yellow tops and hands them to me.

I don't know how to tell her I haven't shopped in a real store for ages. I hold the tops close. They smell new.

I need new so bad.

"Shorts," Lexie says, and we head over to another rack. I go through them slowly because I pretty much want them all. I hold up a pair of bright white shorts, figuring she'll say they're not practical. Reba was always saying that.

"Try them on," Lexie says.

I head to a big room with mirrors, where lots of women are trying on clothes. One lady is in a badly fitting pink dress and I want to tell her, *Don't buy it. You look awful.*

I feel like I've got the sign over my forehead: HOMELESS GIRL.

I take extra care with what I'm trying on. I fold the clothes I'm wearing neatly on a bench. I try on the white shorts and they feel so good. Two of the yellow tops fit funny, but the last one I put on, it's like it was waiting for me to find it.

I look at myself in the mirror, I run my fingers through my hair, and then I turn away because I'm crying.

"You look so pretty," the lady in the bad pink dress says to me. I'm not sure she's a good judge of pretty, but I'll take it, so I smile.

"Thank you, ma'am." I wipe my tears and turn around in the mirror, seeing all the angles of this yellow top and how it hangs just right. A lady carrying lots of clothes walks in—she's pretty, like a model. I watch her from the corner of my eye. She puts on belts and scarves and stands in front of the mirror like she owns the world. I stand off to the side and try to copy her, put my hand on my hip, shake out my hair, and look superserious.

She prances back to her changing area and I prance back to mine. Lexie has more clothes for me to try. It seems like it's Christmas and my birthday when I put on this bright pink top. I feel like I can beat the world.

King Cole told me I could do that.

My hair looks scraggly, but right there, Lexie says, "Let me braid it." And she does just that.

I'm here to tell you, I look like a new girl.

25

SHUSH IS HAVING a good time—probably the best time of his whole life. He is jumping straight up in the air and shaking his furry head in freedom. I run around Lexie and Mac's backyard trying to catch him. They've got every kind of flower here, and I'm yelling, "Don't pee on those flowers, Shush! Don't!"

"It's okay," Lexie shouts at me through the kitchen window. "Let him run."

I lie down on the grass and Shush jumps over me. Then he trots over and licks my face until I start laughing.

Do you know how good Chicago grass smells?

I'm not sure I ever want to leave. A hard thing is happening, too. Part of me doesn't want Reba to get out of the hospital yet. I want to stay here with Lexie and Mac.

"I've got cookies," Lexie says. "Just out of the oven."

"Coming." I head inside with Shush.

Do you know how good this kitchen smells?

I stand over the pan of chocolate cookies and breathe deep. Then I think about waiting for Reba on the bench and seeing her face when she finally showed up. My breath catches in my throat.

"Do you think Reba's got to stay in the hospital for a while?" I ask Lexie.

"A week more, they told me."

"Oh." That's not too long a time.

"I know that's got to be hard for you." Lexie hands me a cookie and puts the others on a tray.

I take a bite. It's warm and chewy like a cookie should be. "I like it here."

"And we like having you." She puts her hand on my shoulder. "Just in case you're feeling at odds with that, let me tell you—liking it here doesn't mean you love your mom any less."

"It doesn't?"

"No."

Two men and a lady walk into the kitchen carrying guitars and scoop up the tray of cookies.

"You sing?" Lexie asks me.

"Well . . . kind of . . . I mean, I used to."

Lexie laughs. "That qualifies here. Sugar, meet Dez, Bodie, and Margo."

"We're the band," the tall guy with a ponytail says. They head down the basement steps with the cookies. Shush goes under the kitchen table to hide.

Lexie goes after them. "We need to defend our food, Sugar. Come on."

x x x

This basement I'm in, it's got dark wood walls, and there are microphones set up in the corner by a drum set and a keyboard. A banner hangs behind the microphones: FRESH RIVER. Mac comes down wearing a Fresh River T-shirt. Dez, Bodie, and Margo are tuning their guitars.

Mac, on a harmonica, plays something bluesy. Margo on the bass comes in with a beat that keeps repeating. That beat is so good, I'm moving to it. Lexie sits down at the keyboard and starts playing. Mac taps his foot.

"Yep," says Margo, nodding her head to the beat, and the other two guitar players jump in, then Lexie plays the melody on the piano. The music is so good, I'm clapping along, and then Mac starts singing.

I was sick and tired a living,
I was walking in the desert so dry,
I was stopping to quit and stepping in spit
And couldn't find a place of supply.
But then the words my mama told me
Fell down on me sure and true,
She said, listen now, this isn't going to last,
'Cause you're just passing through.

They were all singing now in harmony.

And yes, we're just passing through, oh Mama,
We're just passing through.
So take a load off your feet and sing it out sweet,
'Cause we're just passing through.

I love this song!

Mac stops playing and says, "Bodie, I need you to go higher on that riff on the chorus." Bodie plays his guitar part higher, twirls around, and Mac starts singing,

Climb out of your rut
and get off your butt
and suck in your gut

I'm laughing now at the crazy words and now I'm singing with them.

And yes, we're just passing through, oh Mama,
We're just passing through.
So take a load off your feet and sing it out sweet,
'Cause we're just passing through.

Lexie looks at me grinning. "You like that song, Sugar? Mac wrote it."

"I love it."

The band practices some more. I sit here feeling happy, listening to their music. Reba doesn't sing too well, but she loves to dance, and I picture her all new inside, dancing across the floor with Shush in her arms.

But Reba's not dancing free, she's in a locked place. I don't think I can feel happy knowing that.

You know what it's like to move from being happy to being not? It's like swinging as high as you can and someone stops you as you come back down.

"I love your band," I say. "But I'm tired. I'm going upstairs."

I don't know why being happy is so easy to lose.

x x x

I'm lying on my stomach on the white bed in the pink bedroom. I put a dog treat on the rug, waiting; finally Shush's head pokes out from the white bed ruffle. He grabs the treat and goes back to hiding.

"So, do you think about your mother?" I ask him. "Do you think about the place where you used to be? I do." I pull up the ruffle and look at him lying there. "Do you remember our old house? I remember painting the porch with Reba and King Cole. I remember all my birthday parties in the backyard. Reba always went full-out with those. You weren't there for a party."

I'm having trouble breathing, and I need to be quiet or else this could move into an all-out panic attack.

I close my eyes and feel like a drum is pounding in my chest. I try to think of sweet things, like sitting on the front porch harmonizing with King Cole, like catching fireflies with Reba. Fireflies would perch on her hand and stay there for the longest time. "You glow, little one," she'd whisper to them. I wish I could catch a firefly and bring it to her in the hospital.

Shush's head pokes out and he whines a little, which

means he wants to come up with me. I check his paws to make sure he's not dirty. This is a white bed, after all.

"Okay. You can come up." I lift him, and he settles right into the crook of my arm. "It's good here, huh?"

He closes his eyes.

"Here's the problem with the world, as I see it. People try to fit you into their box and say, this is normal, this isn't. People could look at you and say you're a messed-up dog, but you're just sensitive." Shush is looking at me. "If you were just a regular dog, who needed three walks a day and barked all the time, I couldn't keep you. See, you fit with me and Reba." I stroke his head. "Do you miss her? Yeah, me, too."

Shush sniffs my hair. "This is a braid. Don't chew on it."

He looks at me a little strangely.

"I look different, huh? I look like I can beat the world. Right?" I look in the mirror, superserious, like that model lady did. "Beating the world is easier said than done," I add.

Shush sighs and puts his head on my shoulder.

"Change is good," I tell him. "Some change, that is." I hum the passing-through song.

x x x

The next morning I go to see Reba, still humming the song. Dana Wood is with me.

"It will take a few more weeks for your mom's medicine to start working, Sugar."

Why don't they give her medicine that works faster?

I sit with my mother. We don't talk much, I just hold her hand and let her know I'm here.

Reba sighs from this private place in her heart.

"You'll get out of here," I tell her.

"When Mr. Leeland comes—"

"No!" I shout. "You remember the monster at the door?"

She looks down, shaking her head.

I put my face close. "You remember? The man who came about the money?"

I look at my mother sitting on the bed. "Don't forget that, Reba."

She closes her eyes, presses her lips together hard, and nods, but something tells me I'm going to have to keep reminding her. The trick with monsters is they know how to hide.

"I'm tired," Reba says. I cover her with a sheet and kiss her cheek.

Don't give up, Reba. Don't.

I've learned something about sadness this last year. Sometimes the best thing you can do is just sit with someone who's hurting; you don't have to say anything or offer advice, you just sit there.

I think dogs understand this better than people.

So all that week I sit with Reba in the hospital, and I realize that I want to help people more than I want to do anything else. She gets a little better, too. I keep remembering King Cole's favorite hockey movie and what the coach said to the players right before their big Olympic game. So I tell her, "I know things don't look so good right now, but you've got to believe that this is your time, this is your day to win, you've got to gather up what you've got because today you are the greatest woman in America! Now go out there and do it!"

"What?" Reba says.

Maybe that was overkill, but I hope some of it sinks in.

26

"TRY TO LET this sink in," I tell Shush, "because not every dog has a calling. You do."

I show him what I found on the Internet about helper dogs.

"This might seem like a lot at once, but the first thing we've got to do is help you learn to walk across busy streets and not get stressed by the horns and the garbage trucks. Then you need to go into a hospital and handle all the background noise there. Then comes the good part. We go to rooms where people really need a hug from a fur ball. That's you—you're the fur ball. And in those places, you just do your thing—wag your tail and make people feel special. You can do that."

Shush purrs.

I put the leash on him and he sits down. I slap my thigh twice, which is his signal to heel, but he digs in his heels and doesn't move.

"No." I slap my thigh again. "Heel."

He's not going there.

"Dogs like to walk," I mention.

Not this dog. I pick him up and carry him outside. I get him across the street. An old man and his old dog are sitting on a porch. For some reason Shush starts pulling toward them. The old dog lifts his head, Shush sits right at the foot of the porch steps. The old dog rises.

"Now, I've not seen Merlin show much interest in things of late," the old man says to me. "Merlin, you like this little dog?"

This old dog Merlin gets up slow and Shush heads up the stairs. Shush starts sniffing Merlin, and Merlin doesn't seem to mind. The old man asks me, "You walk dogs?"

"I walk mine." I cough. "Not all that well, but I walk him."

"Think you could handle two? I can't walk him anymore."

"I don't know. I could try."

He throws a chewed-up leash to me. I put it around Merlin's neck. "Come on," I say.

Merlin looks at me like Shush does.

"Does he heel?" I ask the old man.

He chuckles. "Obviously not."

I'm getting sick of dogs not obeying me, since I've got the brainpower in the relationship. I yank Shush and Merlin's leashes at the same time. "We're going."

Merlin walks forward a little.

"Good dog." I look at Shush, who's decided to lie down. "Your turn."

Shush starts purring.

"Nice try." I give his leash a quick tug and he's up now. Merlin heads down the steps.

Don't make me look bad, you guys. We head down the block. The problem with walking two dogs is when one stops, the other one wants to keep going. I must look like a real case, but we get to the end of the block and come back in front of the old man's house.

"We didn't get too far," I admit.

"I haven't gotten him that far in years. You come by tomorrow this time and do the same thing. There's money in it for you."

"Yessir!"

"I'm T. A. Cockburn."

"Sugar Mae Cole."

Merlin looks exhausted, like he's just run a race. He lies back down in the exact same spot and closes his eyes.

Mr. Cockburn smiles like he knows a good secret. "Old Merlin here, he keeps the monsters away." He winks at me. "You know?"

More than you know, Mr. Cockburn.

x x x

I walk/carry Shush as far as Saint Mary's Catholic Church, three blocks away. A big bus rumbles by. That does Shush in—he's whining and shaking.

"You want a break?"

I put my green bag down, make the *click click* sound, and he crawls in.

"I think you should feel good about getting this far."

The church door has a sign, ALL ARE WELCOME. I'm going to take them at their word.

"We're not Catholic," I say to Shush, "but we'll try not to let it show."

I head up the stone steps and open the heavy door.

It's so quiet in here, like the rush and noise of the city disappeared. I stand by a stained-glass window, soaking up the quiet. An angel statue hangs on the wall. I look up at this angel's pretty, peaceful face.

Between you and me, I'd rather have an angel look like Iron Man.

I walk over to a table with little candles. I pick a long match, light a small candle in the back of the table. The flame shoots up for just a second.

Dear God, please show the doctors how to help Reba. Make her strong like she used to be.

A few of the candles are smoking, but Reba's flame looks strong.

There's a box, FOR THE POOR.

I'm poor, but I put a quarter in anyway.

There's an old woman sitting on a bench praying. Her head is bowed. She seems to know what she's doing. I go over and tap her on the shoulder.

"Would you pray for my mom?" I ask.

She looks up. *"¿Qué dijo?"*

I should have paid better attention in Spanish class.

"Um," I begin. *"Mi, uh, mi madre es . . ."*

"Enferma . . . ?"

That's close enough. *"Gracias, señor,"* I say. "I mean, *señorita."*

She smiles. *"No señorita—señora."*

She bows her head and gets back to praying.

I walk out of the church, feel Shush at peace in the bag.

I wonder why Lexie takes in kids like me.

I wonder how long I can stay with her and Mac.

I wish when Reba gets out, she could stay at Lexie's, too. But that's not how it works. When Reba gets out, it's not going to be easy. She's going to have to live in a shelter, that's what Dana Wood said.

I'm not sure how to be with that.

27

THIS WAY TO THE WOOZ

Those words are on yellow paper taped to a tree on Lexie's street.

THE WOOZ IS IN

That's in front of a house with a broken-down porch. A fat cat sits in the window. I am walking, or more like dragging Merlin and Shush for their walk. I think by the time this is over my arms are going to be much longer.

Shush is pulling on the leash to get across the street to Lexie's, back to his safe spot. Merlin is pulling the opposite way, toward his house.

"Heel," I say in my best alpha female voice, and both dogs look at me, like, *You're kidding, right?*

A girl about my age comes out on the broken-down porch. She's got straight strawberry blonde hair and a nose so small it hardly matters. "Your dog doesn't like the street, does he?"

"No." Shush is yanking so hard, I'm worried about his neck. "Sit!" I shout.

This girl sits. Shush does, too.

"I hope he's paying you enough," she says.

Me, too.

Shush is looking across the street to Lexie's like it's the only place on earth without a monster.

"My little brother's like that, too, except he's not on a leash. At least, not yet." She sits there thinking. The fat cat in the window seems to be thinking, too. "You're staying with Lexie, aren't you?"

"Yeah."

"I know," she says.

I'm not sure what that means.

"It's okay," she says.

I look down.

"We've all got stuff," she adds.

I don't ask about her stuff.

"I'm Joonie."

"Sugar." I wait for her to laugh. She doesn't.

"So, I bet everybody remembers you, right?"

"Right." Merlin now is fixated on a squirrel and Shush is yanking me toward a bush. "Sit!" I scream.

She laughs. "I'm sitting."

I'm close to getting pulled apart. I drag Merlin back. "You're old," I tell him. "You're supposed to be weak."

I look at the yellow paper on the tree: THE WOOZ IS IN. "Is that your tree?"

She nods. Shush pees on the tree.

I'm trying to get a breath.

"So, what's a wooz?"

She motions me over. "Have you heard about the land of Ziddo, Sugar? Of course you haven't. I just created it last week."

I'm trying to follow this. Shush has stopped pulling. He's sitting, watching this girl. Merlin moves closer to the squirrel.

"On the planet Ziddo all children can trust their parents, because all parents have gone to PE class—that's parent education. They have to get at least a C-plus or they have to repeat the class again."

I picture Mr. Leeland flunking and repeating.

"PE," she continues, "includes, but is not limited to . . . love, continuing care, financial accountability, compassion, and just new in the brochure, anger management. My dad failed big-time at that." She waits.

"You made this up?"

She nods. "Last summer I went to gifted-and-talented camp. My mom can't afford to send me this year, so she's unleashing me on an unsuspecting public." She holds out her hand to Shush, and he sniffs it.

She still didn't answer my question. "What's a wooz?"

"There's only one, the Wise One Of Ziddo."

"That's you?"

She smiles; her braces shine in the light. "You can ask Lexie about me. I'm weird, but I mean well." She heads inside.

I get Merlin to Mr. Cockburn's house three doors down. He's waiting for us.

"Was that fun?" he asks his old dog.

Merlin sighs and Mr. Cockburn hands me ten dollars.

Now, that's fun!

28

FUN HASN'T VISITED Reba in a long time.

The walls in this new place she's at are muddy green, two old beds are in the corners, a sign on the wall says TODAY IS A NEW DAY, which seems kind of obvious. I lay Reba's shoes against the wall as she sits on the bed like she's been in an accident. They were crazy to let her out of the hospital—she's not ready.

"It's okay," I tell her, but it's not okay. It's another shelter, better than Grace Place, but still . . .

"We've got to be strong," I tell Reba. And I read from page twenty-seven of *Upon These Truths I Stand.*

> My daddy always told me that weakness isn't something to be ashamed of. I didn't know what he was talking about until I was older and had had my share of weak moments and mess-ups.

The thing you've got to avoid like an army of wasps flying straight to get you, is giving up. You can't do it, you can't allow it in your heart. You've got to push past your feeling, push past what things look like, push past all your fear, and say, no sir. I'm getting up on my feet. It's a new day,

When I played football, I'd get hit and fall down plenty of times, and the word that came into my head every time was rise. You rise up, boy. You get on your feet and face the thing that knocked you down.

Remember—you heard it here first.

Reba keeps sitting there, but I get up on my feet and unpack the rest of her stuff and fold it nice and put it in a scratched chest of drawers.

There's a knock on the door. Dana Wood comes in. I smile at Reba. "You want me to copy down what I just read to you?"

She shakes her head.

"It's no bother."

She doesn't want it.

You've got to hold on to something, Reba.

She grabs my hand. And now my bag is moving.

Dana Wood stares at me. "You didn't."

Well, actually . . .

I put down my green bag and Shush jumps out. Reba's face breaks into joy like a little kid's. Shush runs right to her, leaps onto her lap, and licks her chin.

"Little one," she says, and buries her face in his soft fur.

Dana Wood crosses her arms, superstrict.

"He's going to be a helper dog," I remind her, and point to Reba, who's laughing, which didn't happen, I bet, at the hospital for emotions with all those experts in charge. "He's going to be one of the great ones," I add, and Shush starts purring.

Sometimes the best thing that can happen to a person is to have a puppy lick your face. Remember, you heard it here first.

x x x

Reba's first assignment at the shelter is to get a part-time job. She says she isn't ready. I think she's right.

"Maybe you could work two days a week," I mention.

She seems scared of the world, like Shush. I'm not proud of this, but sometimes when I visit her, I can't wait to leave and get back to my good life.

I mention this to Joonie, who says, "You can't be in charge of your mother."

"I know that!"

"If she doesn't get a job, it's not your fault. It doesn't mean you failed her."

"I know that!"

Sort of.

Dear Sugar,

I have to tell you—I really miss reading your writing. For the last week of school I gave an assignment to the class:

Write about a dream you have. It can be one you had while you were asleep or a dream you had about something you want to achieve.

Now, a teacher stalking you with homework after you've moved is terribly unfair, I know, but would you like to write something for me on this?

I would love to read it. Claus and I await your reply.

Mr. B

I write him back.

Mr. B, I don't know if I can.

He writes me back.

TRY.

He signs it T.G.B.K.A. (The Great B Knows All).

I visit Reba the next day at the shelter and show her the e-mail.

"Did you write it?" she asks.

Her roommate Henrietta blows her nose. "Of course she did."

And I read them my poem.

Sometimes at night here, I don't want to go to sleep.
I want to memorize every part of the pink bedroom I'm staying in,
Every bit of how the soft sheet feels.
I want to keep it all in my heart for when I have to leave.
I know it's not forever here.
I want a forever place to be.

I wonder if that's a place with walls and a
garden,
Or if it's a place that I always carry in my heart.
I dream of singing happy songs.
I dream of running and not stopping.
I dream of omelettes with too much cheese,
Too many cookies cooling on a counter,
Too many people I love all in the same place—
Even the ones who have left—they are back with
me again.
I want my mother to remember who she is.
I want to find my voice in the world.
And when I do, I want to come back
to the people who have lost their voices
And help them.
I can carry a lot in my pack.
The best thing about dreams is they're not heavy.
I carry them on my shoulders
And in my heart
And balance them on my head.
I let them follow me around, sniffing at my feet,
climbing in my lap and licking my face.
You know, like the best dogs do.

I stand there holding the dream poem. Henrietta is smiling, Reba's eyes are wet.

"That's beautiful, my girl."

I look down, smiling.

"I want you to trust me again," she says softly.

I'm not sure what to say except, "I trust you."

She shakes her head. "I want you to know that I can take care of you. I can stay on my feet. I can turn this thing around. I am determined to do that."

Henrietta's eyes are wet now. "How did you learn to write like that, Sugar?"

"Reba taught me."

She shakes her head. "I did not."

"Yes you did. You were always writing thank-you cards to people, always looking for just the right words to say what was in your heart." I hand her the poem. "You taught me."

x x x

It's written on plain white paper, and she apologized for that.

But the envelope with the pretty handwriting shows up at Lexie's two days later, addressed to me.

Dear Sugar,

I am amazed at your grace and your courage.

I am blessed by how you go through the world.

I don't know what I did to deserve a daughter like you, but I'm not going to question it, I'm just going to enjoy the gift. I would imagine that your brand of moxie, smarts, and talent is going to turn a portion of this sour old world on its ear.

Sugar Mae Cole, you embody the best kind of sweetness.

I intend to be the kind of mother you deserve. And when I have one of those days where I'm not doing anybody much good, you have my permission to shove this letter in my face and remind me of what I promised.

Watch this space, girl, because I'm coming back!

With love,

Reba

I sit with the letter. I have plastic wrap to cover it, but I don't want to cover it just yet. I want to soak up all that it says.

29

WE HEREBY DECLARE THE FIRST LAWS OF ZIDDO:

CREATURES ARE TO BE GIVEN RIGHT OF WAY.

ALL BEINGS ARE ENCOURAGED TO LIVE IN HARMONY.

VIOLENCE AND MEANNESS ARE SO NOT TOLERATED.

WE HOPE YOU ENJOY YOUR VISIT HERE.

AND, YES, YOU ARE BEING WATCHED BY THE CREATURE

WITH FORTY-SEVEN DAGGERS WHO IS EASILY IRRITATED.

THIS MESSAGE IS BROUGHT TO YOU BY

THE WOOZ (WISE ONE OF ZIDDO) AND COMPANY

I am sitting on Joonie's front steps when the fattest cat I've ever seen waddles up.

"Butterbutt," Joonie says, "this is Sugar."

I laugh. "Butterbutt?"

"He sat on a stick of butter when he was little, and it took forever to clean him up."

Butterbutt looks at me, not impressed.

The feeling is mutual.

A lady walks out, miserable. "Tell me I can go into my office and work effectively even though I am working at home. Tell me I can do this without eating half a bag of cookies."

"What kind of cookies?" Joonie asks.

"The almond butter ones."

Joonie stands up. "Don't eat them, Helen!"

"I really prefer it when you call me Mom. Maybe I'll go get coffee." She shakes my hand. "Welcome to our porch."

"You can go into your office and work effectively even though you're working at home," Joonie tells her.

"You're lying." Helen walks down the street.

"The Wooz does not lie." Joonie looks down. "Helen has more courage than she knows."

"My mom does, too."

She reaches out to pet Butterbutt, who steps back. "I sense you and I have things in common, Sugar. Fatherwise, I mean."

I'm not sure if I should ask. "What did your dad do?"

Joonie stretches out her arms to the sky and leans back. "Ah, my father, Hargrove Merman the Third, well, he did many things. He cheated on my mother, he made Illinois' list of top deadbeat dads, and his face was on television."

A little boy wearing spaceship pajamas comes out of the house reading a book with a whale on the cover.

"I'm sorry," I say.

She smiles sadly. "There's a warrant out for his arrest."

The boy focuses on his book.

I smile. "Send the creature with forty-seven daggers."

"In this case, the creature might lose."

"Our dad knows how to hide," the boy says. He shows a picture of a whale diving deep under the water. "Like this."

I nod. "My dad knows how to hide, too."

"Maybe they know each other."

Maybe . . .

Joonie sits there, thinking. "When's the last time you saw your dad, Sugar?"

"At my grandfather's funeral. He said we were going to be a real family, and then he left town."

Joonie pushes back her bangs like nothing I say could shock her.

"What was the best thing about him, Sugar?"

I never once thought of that. "I guess the way he made Reba laugh."

Joonie crosses her arms across her chest. "Hargrove Merman the Third makes the best pancakes in the world. Right, Chandler?"

"With blueberries," the boy adds. "And real maple syrup."

Mr. Leeland made gumbo and corn bread. Reba talked about it a lot, but I only had it once.

I stand up. "I need to go see my mom."

"Tell her she's brave," Joonie says.

I smile. "I will."

30

AND I DO.

Reba puts down her book.

"Real brave," I add.

She starts smiling. "You think so?"

Me and the Wooz think so.

"I know so."

"You came all the way down here on the bus to tell me that?"

I put down my green bag. It moves a little.

She laughs. "You brought company?"

I make sure the door to her room is closed and then I let Shush out. He sees Reba and his little stump of a tail goes wild.

"Little one, look at you!" Reba picks him up and rocks him like a baby. Shush licks her face and she's laughing. "Yes, I know," she says to him. "I know. It's wonderful to see you, too." She takes my hand. "Sugar Mae Cole, you beat all."

I grin. *I sure try.*

She grins. "I want you to know something, Sugar. I almost called Mr. Leeland, but I didn't."

My mouth feels dry. "Why did you want to call him? He doesn't help."

She sits on the floor with Shush and rubs his tummy. "I'm working with a therapist to understand why."

I hope you work real hard, Reba.

She's humming to Shush. There's peace on her face. Shush rolls on his back to get more of his tummy rubbed. Reba laughs—she's got the best laugh—and rubs him.

x x x

Shush's visit does so much for Reba that in a week she finds herself a part-time job cleaning houses.

"That's a very important step," Dana Wood says.

Reba keeps stepping out, too. Her medicine is making her feel better.

She starts exercising a little.

She's taking vitamins, and her face looks rosier.

My face is red, at least that's what Joonie says. Red from trying to walk Merlin and Shush.

Thanks to Dante, I have another old dog to walk—Puffypoo. I'm not kidding. And if you think Merlin has issues . . .

"Puffypoo," I say, "I'm here to help you."

Puffypoo snarls and looks away. I'm not going to take this personally. I bring Shush up on the porch to meet her. "See, here's your new little friend." Shush sniffs Puffypoo while she yawns. "And we're all going to walk together and pray I survive." I give her leash a tug. "So, come on. Get up."

Puffypoo's owner, Mrs. Hester, is watching this from her rocking chair. "She won't do much, I told you she won't do much."

I look at Shush. "Anything you could do to help would be good right now."

Shush looks at Puffypoo and whines. That gets Puffypoo up.

"Good dogs!"

Shush whines some more and Puffypoo starts whining, too. Merlin throws back his head and yelps.

Mrs. Hester is laughing and rocking. I shriek, "Heel," and not one of the three dogs pays attention, but it seems that three dogs move better than two dogs. Right now Shush is in the lead.

Now Merlin is in the lead.

Now Puffypoo sits down and refuses to go anywhere.

Shush starts to whine, Merlin yelps, and Puffypoo moves slowly down the street. "I hope they're paying you enough," Joonie says.

Dante is coming toward me with another dog on the leash.

I shake my head. "Three's my limit."

"It's more money."

"I'll be dead."

Dante smiles. "This is Greg." The dog looks at me.

What kind of a name is that?

Puffypoo trots over to Greg and sniffs his nose, and Greg seems to like that. Then Shush wants in on this and he trots over, but Puffypoo snarls at him, Shush backs off. Merlin yelps.

"More money," Dante says, handing me Greg's leash.

"Help me."

"I work better with plants."

X X X

Reba comes to help me, and Merlin falls in love with her.

"That dog's breath," she says, turning away.

We head to the park with Merlin in the lead, and as long as Greg goes forward, Puffypoo isn't far behind. Shush is mostly interested in stopping today. Then Merlin goes left and Greg goes right, causing their leashes to get tangled with another dog, who starts yipping; then Puffypoo almost attacks a puppy, but not quite, because Reba, thinking quick, screams, "Back off from that baby!" Then Greg steals a man's sandwich, jumping up and tearing it out of the guy's hand while he's sitting on a bench; Greg gulps it down as the poor man starts screaming, but Reba knows how to handle these things.

"I am shocked, sir, that you've lost your lunch. Please accept my apology. This is not my dog, he is not trained in the finer things, and I am so sorry that he stole your . . . what was it?"

"Meatball sub with melted mozzarella and extra peppers," the man says miserably.

A few minutes later, Greg pukes it up.

Reba looks at the puke on the grass and tells Greg, "I hope you've learned your lesson."

I split the money with her at the end of the walk. "You want to do this tomorrow?"

Reba sits on Lexie's steps fanning herself. "I do not."

31

"MY MOTHER USED to say painting a room a fine color is the number one cheapest thing a woman can do to be transformed."

Lexie is standing by a sign, COLOR CHANGES EVERYTHING. The wall in front of her has different paint samples. Every color in the world is here.

"I'm looking for something exciting," she tells me. "And this isn't easy because Mac thinks brown is exciting." Lexie picks up a sheet of yellow colors and holds it to the light. Those look pretty exciting to me, but Lexie shakes her head. "I need bolder."

"Purple?" I ask.

She laughs. "I'd love it. Mac would kill me." She's holding different paint sheets up. She gets to orange and stops. "I love this. Tangerine Mist."

"Wouldn't Mac kill you for that?"

"He'd only think about it. I'm getting a sample. You ever paint a room?"

"I've painted a porch and a door."

"Then you're not an amateur."

I'm standing by the blues—there are so many blues. I had a blue bedroom once. I pick out a paint sample sheet with cobalt blue. I'd love a house where each room is a different bright color. I'd have a cobalt blue hallway. The minute people walk in, they'd feel the electricity.

"You can take some paint cards if you want," Lexie tells me. "They're free."

I grab blues, greens, and purples—peacock colors. King Cole gave me a peacock feather once, but I lost it after we got kicked out of our house. He told me a peacock has about two hundred feathers.

I said, "No wonder they're so proud."

"I'm not sure they're proud as much as they know what they've been given and they're not ashamed to show it."

x x x

"Here's what you've been given," I tell Shush.

He's hiding under the table. I'm on my knees looking at him.

"See, you're cute beyond words, you're a very good hugger, and even though you had a hard time, you're still brave. Most of the time." I put a treat on the floor. "If you want to come over, you can."

Shush doesn't move. He's much braver around his dog friends.

I push the treat closer. Shush sniffs the air. "That's food, and you've got to go for it, you know? You can't just hide under the table. You've got people around you who want to help. Not every dog has that."

Shush puts his head down and closes his eyes.

"There's a peacock in you," I mention.

"You know who would have loved this dog?" It's Lexie, lugging a ladder from the basement. "My girl Tonya. She loved every animal God ever made. She'd bring dead birds in here and try to revive them."

I help her with the ladder. We bring it into the little office.

"Tonya came to us after her father had been arrested. She was thirteen years old; she stayed here for seven months."

"I didn't know kids could stay that long."

"Oh, yes. But she ran away; snuck out in the middle of the night. I didn't see it coming. If I had . . ."

Lexie hands me a piece of sandpaper, so sad.

"Everything on this earth was against Tonya. Her dad was in jail; her mom didn't want her; she hated herself: she was on and off drugs."

"We did everything we could." Mac is standing at the door.

Lexie shakes her head. "We missed the signs. We could have kept her safe. I just needed to work with her a little longer."

Mac shakes his head. "Tonya didn't want to be safe, babe."

"She didn't know she could be safe, Mac! Why can't you get that?"

Shush trots up to Lexie and sits by her feet. He can tell when people are hurting. He whines a little. She bends down, grinning.

"You're one special dog, do you know that?"

Yeah, he knows that. Shush wags his stump of a tail and sticks out his pink tongue.

Lexie puts her hands on her hips and looks around the room. "We're going to make a bold statement in here." She starts covering the furniture with plastic.

I look at the sandpaper. "What do I do with this?"

"You rub, honey. You rub out all the imperfections

in that wall and get it ready for new life."

There are a lot of dents in this wall.

"Take it one dent at a time," she says, and I start rubbing.

I'm on my knees, getting to it.

I like the feel of sandpaper in my hand.

I like how it feels to smooth things out.

It turns out, I'm a good rubber. It's a natural gift I have. Shush comes over and sniffs the wall.

"See how quick things get better?" I tell him.

We rub, and Lexie tells me about when she and her mom and sister had to sleep in their car in the park. "We did it for two months, so I know, Sugar. I know about being on the street. My grades went south and I just about up and died from all the stress. I got a high fever of one hundred and four and I ended up in the ER." She laughs. "That fever didn't want to go, either, but it was the best thing that could have happened."

Was she kidding? "Why?"

"I met Dr. Hester. He'd come in to visit me in my hospital room and we'd get to talking. He told me, 'Lexie, you've got the stuff to have a good life.' I told him he was crazy. He said, 'I was fourth in my class at Cornell Medical School, and I know what I'm talking about.'

He said I had strengths I didn't see. I was a good communicator, I was good with people, I had a warm way about me."

"You really do," I tell her.

"'I'm betting you're not going to be a statistic,'" he told me. "'You know how to survive. Do better than that. Go out there and thrive.'" She goes after a big scratch with the sandpaper.

"That's what I want to do," I say quietly, just in case it sounds dumb. But I feel it so strong, I say it again.

"I want to do that, too. I want to have a good life!"

Lexie is standing on a ladder, rubbing. "Now, I don't have a degree from Cornell, but I've got one in street smarts, and I can tell you, Sugar, you're the finest girl we've had through here yet."

"Thank you," I whisper.

I rub even harder.

"Don't put a hole through the wall."

I grin. "Sorry."

There are dents that need something called Spackle, which is like paste that fills in cracks. Lexie shows me how to put the Spackle in. I smooth it out.

"When do we paint, Lexie?"

"Oh, not yet. It's got to dry."

I'm wondering about Tonya—where she is now. So I ask.

"Well," Lexie tells me, "she didn't make it. She overdosed. They found her dead in Pittsburgh two days before her fourteenth birthday."

She heads out of the room.

Man.

"I'm sorry, Lexie, I shouldn't have asked, I . . ."

Lexie turns back and looks at me, fierce. "You just stay off those drugs, you hear me?"

"I've never—"

She points a finger at me, her eyes fill with pain. "I'm not saying you have, Sugar, but drugs are out there, and they're looking for kids to destroy. Anybody comes at you with them, you act like they've just stuck a king cobra snake in your face. You get me? You run, girl! There's nothing cute about it, nothing cool about it, all the promises you'll feel good—it's all smoke. You'll never feel worse than you do on drugs. You could end up like Tonya—stone cold dead. You've been pretty lucky in this world—most of the kids we get through here have had a much tougher time."

32

LEXIE AND I put tape around the windows and the door, and we take off the electrical covers. I'm feeling grateful to be here, grateful to not be in a deeper mess than I already am.

"Do we paint now?" I ask.

"Not yet."

We use a vacuum and get up all the dust, we wash the walls with a sponge, we wipe everything down with water.

Shush is in the kitchen behind a gate, whining. He wants to help.

"There are things a dog can't do," I tell him. He slinks under the table, pouting.

Lexie shows me how to put caulk between the gaps where the molding meets the walls. I smooth that in with a putty knife. We wait some more. I didn't know waiting was such a big part of painting.

"Now," Lexie says, "we paint." She opens the paint can to the most wonderful orange color—Tangerine Mist.

I love painting walls. It's the best feeling. I'm covering the old and bringing in the new. I'm good with the roller because I've got strong arms. Lexie paints the parts around the windows and doors and I roll and fill in with color. I feel like we're making a tangerine grove right here.

I feel like the sun is shining right on this room.

I feel happier than I've felt in I don't know when.

And when it's over, I lie down on the floor and look at the glowing orange walls with the white trim and start laughing.

"I want to paint my whole life over with tangerine," I tell her.

Lexie looks around the room grinning and says, "Mac's going to kill me."

"Why's that?" Mac's standing at the door with the band. He gulps. "It's bright."

I nod.

"It's really . . . orange . . ." Bodie says.

"Tangerine Mist," Lexie says. "You said I could pick any color."

Margo nods. She likes it. The men cough and walk off.

"He'll get used to it," Lexie whispers to me.

I'm used to it now! It's the same room, but entirely new. I'm going to be a girl like that—entirely new.

I hear the band tuning up. Lexie shakes her head. "You know, we almost stopped playing together."

"Why?"

"Well, some people wanted to try to make it big and others wanted to take it easy, play the gigs that came along."

"What did you want?"

She laughs. "We work hard enough at the landscaping business. I wanted it easy."

x x x

A few hours later, there's something in this orange room I've not seen before—a dollhouse.

I kneel down to look at it. It's two stories tall with furniture in every room. There's even a little bathroom with a sink and tub—no toilet, though.

I guess dolls don't have to go.

"Mac made it for me," Lexie explains. "Our thirtieth

anniversary is coming up in August. I always wanted one of these."

I move closer to it. On the first floor, there's a toy dog lying in front of a fireplace.

On the top floor, a toy cat sits on a bed. The sign over the front door says HOME SWEET HOME.

It's just a big thing to play with—I know that.

Lots of homes aren't close to sweet—I know that, too.

But this little house seems so good and safe.

There's a father doll on the porch. The mother is in the living room. There are kid dolls of different skin colors in the bedrooms.

"You can touch it, Sugar."

I take one of the kid dolls and bring her down the steps.

I wonder when Papa will be home.

I'm not sure where that came from—probably a book. I never called my father anything but Mr. Leeland.

I bring the girl doll into the kitchen.

I'm going to surprise Mama and Papa and make them chocolate chip pancakes. This is no big deal for me. I'm an ace at this.

I move the girl doll into the kitchen and bring in the father doll to say something nice to her.

I bite my lip. I can't think of what he'd say.

Well, aren't you a sight for sore eyes?

Mr. Leeland usually said that to me. I never quite knew if it was a compliment or not.

I would have come by sooner, but I got caught up with business.

Mr. Leeland used to say that, too. Business for him was gambling.

I sit back on my heels and cross my arms tight.

I'm too old to be playing dollhouse.

Lexie is licking stamps and putting them on post cards. "My life didn't get good till I met Mac. He put in so much work on that dollhouse. Look, it even has little pictures on the walls." I peer into the rooms. "You can come in here anytime you want, Sugar."

I touch the little porch rail, remember Reba sitting in her white chair on our old porch drinking iced tea, remember those last scary months when she was talking on her pink phone, clutching the little silver bell necklace.

I hug my knees and look at this little house and want to become a miniature me and crawl inside. I look at

Lexie, who has so much peace it doesn't seem like she ever had trouble in life. I don't know why I want her to know this, but I do.

"I write poems sometimes."

"You do?"

"Maybe I could show you one."

"I would like that."

I know the one to start with. I race up the stairs, past the photos on the wall, past the torn wallpaper.

I get my writing folder and find the poem I wrote in Mr. B's class about bad persuasion. I head back down and hand it to her.

There are people in our lives we cannot trust.
One of those people in my life is my father.

She reads it a few times, nodding, then she hugs me strong. It's one of those times when you don't need words, but I know she's got some broken places, like me. I hang on to her with everything I've got.

33

"WILL YOU BE deciding anytime this week?"

The lady behind the counter at the Sweet Spot asks me this. I feel instantly stupid.

There are cashew caramel delights, hand-dipped chocolate graham crackers, white chocolate logs, peanut-butter milk chocolate crunch bars, coconut cream balls, fruit and nut squares, chocolate mint cups—and that's just the front row.

I haven't had choices like this in I don't know how long.

"Take your time," Lexie whispers to me.

A man waits behind us. "Go ahead, sir," I tell him.

All the time I was homeless I'd look in windows wanting to be one of the people inside. Now I'm inside, and I can't decide.

"How's it going for you, Mildred?" Lexie asks the lady behind the counter.

Mildred groans. Her son is out of work and he moved back home with her and her feet are killing her and her landlord isn't fixing the drip in her kitchen ceiling and her neighbor plays loud music all night long and her daughter-in-law has an *attitude*.

This sour lady doesn't know much about sweetness.

When it's my turn again, I smile like Reba taught me to do—from the heart. "I'll have the dark chocolate caramel chew with macadamia nuts, ma'am. Thank you."

Mildred sniffs, puts my candy on a napkin, and hands it to me.

"I'm real sorry about your feet and everything else," I tell her.

She looks down. I bet most people don't say that to her.

Lexie gets a megasized chocolate-covered strawberry. We sit down at a table by the window. I take a bite of my candy. It's so good, I nearly stand up and shout. I've got to come back and get one of these for Reba.

The sun is beaming through the windows. Lexie's wearing a bright shirt worthy of a peacock. A lady with a laptop computer is working in the corner, two mothers with babies in strollers are laughing at the next table over. I start laughing, too.

"What did I miss?" Lexie asks.

How do I tell her?

"It's just . . . well, it's just so normal."

Lexie looks around. "Well, I guess it is."

I lean closer and whisper, "What I mean is, it's normal because I'm sitting inside."

I tell her about the bakery back in Missouri where they'd give away what they didn't sell at the end of each day to street people. But you couldn't come inside to eat, you ate it by the trash compactor.

"They make their own candy bars," Lexie tells me.

I take a small bite. I want to make this last. I didn't know candy bars came like this. "This is one of my best days in a long time," I tell her.

She smiles like she's got the warmth of the sun glowing inside her. "I'm glad, Sugar. Here's hoping those best days start piling up for you."

I need to bring Reba here. She needs a best day bad.

X X X

"If I ever come into money," Reba tells Shush, "this is the kind of house I want, with the wraparound porch and the double front doors."

She holds the copy of *Southern Living* out, and Shush sniffs it.

"Heavens! Look at that garden."

Shush looks and wags his tail.

Reba turns the pages, lost in her dreams. "Can you imagine this porch done up all in green?" She grins and scratches Shush under the chin. "And we could have little cakes out there and drink iced tea. You're a fine little gentleman. Yes, you are." She whispers, "The houses I'm cleaning now? The people aren't keeping them in shape like they should. People have lost the sense of tradition, but you and me, we're not going to lose it."

Shush climbs onto Reba's lap as she reads to him about how to make whoopie pies. "Now, you need real butter and you need to make sure it's soft. . . ."

Lexie walks in with chocolate cookies she bought at the Sweet Spot. Reba takes one, bites in, and nods.

"How long," Reba says, "do you think the state will want Sugar here? I'm just curious."

I don't like that question.

Lexie bites her lip. "That's hard to say."

Reba flips a page. "I was just thinking that since things are going so well for me . . ." She doesn't finish that sentence.

They haven't been going well for very long!

Reba looks at Lexie and smiles a fake smile. "I know you don't have children of your own. I know you're very close to *my* daughter."

Whoa, Reba.

Lexie face gets tight. She sits down. "You have a fine girl here, Reba, and Mac and I are happy to have her stay with us for as long as—"

"You know, sometimes I wonder, do you want Sugar and me to be able to live with one another?"

I march up to her. "What are you saying?"

Shush isn't used to me shouting. He looks scared and confused.

She's going all-out Southern now. "I'm merely asking a general question about propriety and this system and how I can best understand it."

"The goal in all this," Lexie says slowly, "is to reunite parents and children *when it is best*."

Reba puts Shush on the floor. "And who decides that?"

I break in. "Dana Wood. You know that, Reba."

She smiles sweetly. "And maybe a judge."

"That's right," Lexie adds.

"Well, I best be going." She taps the *Southern Living* with her finger, gives Shush a hug, gives me one, too.

I don't like how I'm feeling. It's like something came into this room and left a bad smell. Lexie marches back to the kitchen carrying the cookies.

"I'm sorry she said those things, Lexie. She shouldn't have—"

"It's all right," Lexie snaps.

No, it's not.

If we were near a lake, I think there'd be ripples on the water.

34

THE NEWS AT Joonie's house is complicated. The police found Joonie's dad living in Arizona.

"He told them he didn't have any money to pay all those years of back child support, but he was living in a nice house with his new wife and little son. He got arrested and put in jail," Joonie tells me. "So, I guess, somewhere out there, I have another brother."

I gulp. "It's good they found him."

"I guess. Helen's glad." She rubs Shush. "He's been married four, no, five times now."

"That's a lot."

"Yeah."

Dante sits on the steps. "We don't quite know where my uncle is."

I can relate. Mr. Leeland is somewhere out there, too.

"We could start a Somewhere Out There club," Joonie suggests.

And for some reason I tell them about the fight I overheard when I was in third grade. Mr. Leeland was yelling at Reba that he wasn't ready to be a father and when I came along he couldn't handle the responsibility. He was screaming at her, *You should have been careful. What's the matter with you?* Like he didn't have anything to do with it.

"I changed their whole marriage." Shush sighs and leans against my leg. "Sometimes it feels like I ruined everything."

Joonie shakes her head. "That's not true."

King Cole said that when I told him about it.

"Really not true," Dante adds. "Write that down, Sugar. I'm not kidding."

It's cool to have friends who help you figure out your life.

Chandler comes out on the porch in his pajamas. "Are we going to see Daddy?"

Joonie puts her arm around him. "I don't know. Do you want to?"

Chandler thinks about that. "If we saw him, how would it be?"

Joonie shakes her head. "I don't know." She looks at me and Dante. "Help me out, guys."

Dante clears his throat. "It would probably be a combination of being glad to see him because he's your dad, and feeling a little uncomfortable because he hasn't been around and helping."

Chandler nods and scratches his knee. "Maybe the dragon with forty-seven daggers could fly us over there."

"Maybe," Joonie says.

Shush jumps over Dante's legs and heads right to Chandler. He sits in front of him and wags his tail. Chandler laughs and then he hugs him for a long time.

That's when a silver car drives up the street, and a hand waves from the window. My heart catches in my throat as Mr. Leeland gets out holding a big teddy bear and a box of chocolates, looking handsome like a movie star.

"Well, Miss Sugar. Aren't you a sight for sore eyes?"

I don't say anything, I can't say anything.

Mr. Leeland walks right up to the porch. "Well, I've had better greetings, I'll tell you what."

What do you want from me?

I want to run, but it's like my legs have turned to stone.

"Who's that?" Chandler asks me.

I look down. "This is Mr. Leeland, my father."

Dante gets up and stretches out his hand. "How do you do, sir?"

Mr. Leeland shakes it. "'Bout as well as I can."

x x x

Mr. Leeland sits down in Mac's special chair like it belongs to him. "Reba said she'd meet me here. We're looking at apartments together."

"She didn't tell me that."

He smiles. "Our little surprise."

Lexie brings coffee, Shush trots in and stops.

"Well, hey there, little guy." Mr. Leeland puts his hand out, but Shush backs off.

My father throws a bag to me. I catch it. "I didn't know what to get you, but I remember your mother teaching you about the fine art of gratitude."

Shush sniffs the bag. I open it to a box of cards with sunflowers on them and the words THANK YOU written in gold.

"I remember those sunflowers you grew," he adds.

Okay, this is a pretty good gift, but I'm not getting sucked in. "They're probably dead now."

"Or they've shot up to the sky," he says. "There's a gold pen in there, too."

I find that in the bag. Mac is standing in the doorway now.

Mr. Leeland looks at everybody. "Could my daughter and I talk alone?"

"No," Mac and Lexie say together.

He laughs nervously. "All right then. Sugar, honey, your mother called me and told me what happened. I got here as soon as I could." He looks at his tan hands. "I want to help."

"She needs to keep getting stronger," I tell him.

"And how 'bout you, Sugar? What do you need?"

I look at Lexie, Mac, and Shush.

I need a real house and a normal family.

"I don't need anything," I tell him as Shush licks my cheek.

"I know I have to prove to you and your mother that things can be different."

I sit there not talking.

"You know," he says, "there were good times."

I remember that week in fourth grade when he picked me up from school and took me to a poker game in Boyd Marsh's basement. I had to sit by the boiler waiting for him to lose so we could go home.

I had to tell my teacher the next day, "I didn't get my

homework done, Mrs. Powell, because my father bet a straight and lost to three aces."

"I've taken a room in town," he says.

Me, too. Mine's pink.

That's when Reba shows up. Mac leads her into the living room. Her face breaks into joy. "It isn't!"

Mr. Leeland chuckles and shouts, "Oh, yes it is!"

She runs into his arms and they have the kind of kiss that makes everyone else in the room uncomfortable.

Lexie stands by me and puts her strong hand on my shoulder.

You keep your hand on me, okay? 'Cause I'm going to need it.

When they're done kissing, Reba pulls me away from Lexie. "*We're* your family, miss. Don't you forget that."

35

HE CAME AND he went, my father did. But then he came back.

He came with promises, and Reba believed every one.

Now we're going to be a real family.

Starting now, things are going to change.

He came to Lexie's without calling and brought doughnuts. I didn't want to see him. I didn't have to, but Lexie said she'd be there with me since that was the law.

Mr. Leeland and I sit in the kitchen and eat doughnuts. Lexie is there, too. That's the law of the state of Illinois, supervised visits. Illinois has some good laws.

"Sugar, you don't like me much, do you?" he asks.

How does a kid answer that?

"I don't know you much."

"Well, that's true."

"How come you didn't help us when we lost our house?"

"I tried to get there. I was detained. It killed me not to come."

His voice sounds like he means every word; his eyes fill with love.

I look at him, really look, at his blond hair and his black eyes, and his white-tooth smile and his blue shirt with the sleeves rolled up and his wedding ring on his hand and his jeans and cowboy boots.

And I just get sick of being lied to.

"No sir, I don't think you did." I stand up. "I think you like making promises so people will like you, but you don't know how to keep them much."

"Just a minute, young lady."

I shout, "No, sir, I haven't got a minute."

"I'm full-out tired of this attitude, you hear me? Every day, I'm looking how to win best for me and our family."

You're a loser and you brought us down with you until we had to leave everything we loved.

Lexie is standing now. I look at her and she shoots courage into me. "I don't want to talk anymore," I say.

Mr. Leeland pushes back his chair in disgust. "This isn't much of a system. I'm trying to get to know my daughter and I feel like I've got a crowd around me."

"I understand," Lexie tells him, "but it's the way the system works."

"For now!" He leaves without saying good-bye.

I wanted him to leave. And it hurt me when he did.

I stand there crying. Shush runs up and I hold him close. "I don't know what's the matter with me."

Mac walks in and heads to the refrigerator. "Well, that man is your father, Sugar. And there's love inside you for him, no matter how you feel."

"I don't want there to be any of that. He doesn't deserve any of that!"

"Under the circumstances, I think you're doing pretty darn well. This isn't easy." He opens the refrigerator and gets out two root beers. He gives one to me. I'd forgotten how creamy a root beer tastes.

He sits down at the table, and I do, too.

"We had a drummer who played with us for two years," Mac begins. "He was always late for practice. Sometimes he didn't even show. He was a friend of mine, so I let it go. He was always going around town wearing his Fresh River jacket, telling everyone what a great band we were and how much he loved being part of it. He wasn't fully part of it, and it hurt everybody.

We knew what real commitment looked like and this guy didn't."

"What did you do?"

"At first we let it almost destroy the band, and then we fired him."

Is he telling me to fire my father?

He guzzles his root beer. "What I'm trying to say is it's all right to feel the way you're feeling. If you weren't upset, I'd be worried about you. Your dad, for whatever reason, hasn't really shown you he can be trusted, so why would you trust him?"

Maybe I should be taking notes.

"I would hope," Mac says, "you wouldn't trust him until you had some decent proof he'd changed. From what I can see, your dad loves you. I don't think he loves himself too much. I think he likes easy solutions and might never change. But he loves you. I'd go to the mat on that one."

Shush sniffs the air and leans his head against my chest. I needed that. I rub his good, soft fur.

"I don't usually talk this much," Mac says. "But you're such a fine girl, you listen to me. You've had your share of adults acting badly, but don't give up on us all. It's safe here. You read me?"

"I read you." I look down. "I'm glad you still have the band."

Lexie smiles. "We stopped playing for a year, but we were miserable without our music. We're just starting up again. . . ."

There's a knock on the door. I'm not getting it.

"Hey!" It's Dante's voice. "You want to show me where you want that little tree?"

x x x

"Are you guys going to help or watch me work?"

"Watch," Joonie says.

Dante takes a bag of dirt and lugs it to the trash. Then he lifts a baby tree out of the back of the truck and starts digging a hole.

"How did you learn so much about plants?" I ask him.

"Mac taught me. This little tree here? It can't survive on its own. The wind will knock it down. So we've got to give it support to grow while it's young."

"We need to make this part of parent education on Ziddo," Joonie says.

Dante laughs and puts two posts in the ground, one on either side of the hole. He puts water in the hole and special tree food, then he puts the baby tree in so gently. He fills the hole up, pats it down, and uses wire to connect the little tree to the posts.

"This way, it should make it through winter," he says.

I'm thinking the posts in my life are Mac and Lexie.

"You're in a good place," Dante tells me. He clips some yellow flowers, hands them to me, and digs another hole.

"Hmmmm . . ." Joonie says.

Shush is sniffing the flowers.

I've never had a guy give me flowers. I look at Joonie and mouth, *What should I do?"*

She leans over. "Say thank you and put them in water."

36

I NEED THOSE strong posts to hold me up. The wind here is blowing hard. It feels like winter is coming in the middle of August.

Mr. Leeland and Reba are looking for an apartment. He keeps saying, "We're going to be a real family."

I tell him, "No sir. The state of Illinois wants me here."

"Well," he says, "we'll see about that nonsense. I've got me a lawyer who's going to rattle some cages."

I run upstairs to the pink room and lock the door. I shove a chair in front of it.

I'm not leaving this place!

I get out my pen and write,

Dear State of Illinois,

I want to thank you for having rules that protect kids, and I hope you're superserious about making sure they work. I didn't like that group home I got stuck in when I first came to town. But it was sure better than being on the street, so I'm grateful.

I just want you to know that if Mr. Robert E. Leeland has his lawyer show up and tells you that he wants me to start living with him, you have my permission to start laughing and say, "Suck eggs!" or whatever you think might be appropriate.

Just so you know, I'm not leaving the place where you put me because on the second try, you got it right.

Keep up the good work. I'm counting on you.

Yours very truly,

Sugar Mae Cole

X X X

Five days after Mr. Leeland showed up in Chicago, he left.

Left Reba with all her big dreams of being loved.

"In Cinderella," she says, "the prince doesn't leave town. I guess I keep wanting the fairy tale."

I never liked that story much—I never trusted that prince.

I take her by the hand. "Come on. There's a place I've been wanting to take you."

x x x

The sun is shining through the windows and it seems like the sweetest place on earth. Mildred is complaining about her throbbing veins, but that doesn't matter. Reba looks at the candy and the people and sits down, grinning.

I knew she'd love it.

I buy her two kinds of chocolate and a coffee with steamed milk. I bring them over to the table as Reba studies the place.

"They could do so much more in this room, you know."

I put the coffee down. "Like what?"

"Potted plants, tablecloths." She points outside. "And they could use that porch."

She leans back in her chair. "I'd paint that wall rose and the other wall yellow." She takes a bite of the chocolate and grins. "But I wouldn't change this—not one whit."

It didn't make sense, and I didn't think she'd have the courage to do it, but two days later Reba walked into the Sweet Spot with her makeup just so and her pink shirt and white pants and told Sharon, the owner, "I believe in the power of sweetness. I would love to work here."

She came back grinning and I knew she got the job.

"They can do a lot more with sweetness, in my opinion," Reba says, "and I only gave them a few pointers to get started, like, please, for heaven's sake, use that porch you have for customers. People will talk about things on a porch they'd never discuss inside. It just opens you up. I told her, you should have hanging pots with flowers everywhere, and you should have those walls painted a fresh color."

"Great ideas." Helen passes the salad to me.

We are sitting at Joonie's kitchen table having pizza and salad to celebrate Reba's new job. Helen's idea.

"And then, of course, there's Mildred." Reba sighs. "She is a tired, old soul."

"She's mean," Chandler says.

"She is," Reba agrees, "but there's always a reason for that. You just don't know another person's miseries."

And Reba is telling how Mildred looked her up and

down "like I was something the cat dragged in, but I didn't take it personally. I just smiled at her, and when she told me about her daughter-in-law, well, I told her, 'She's lucky to have a hardworking woman like you as a role model.'"

Helen laughs. "What did Mildred say?"

Reba's chuckling. "Well, she was stunned to silence."

It feels so good sitting in this little kitchen at the lime green table eating pizza and soggy salad. Shush and Butterbutt are at opposite ends of the room staring at each other. We help clean up, then Reba, who normally stays up much later than she should, says, "I've got a mighty big day tomorrow. I best be going."

Shush and I walk Reba to the bus stop. She has to take two buses to get back to the shelter. Shush stops every few feet because of the street noise. Reba bends down and rubs him under the chin.

"You just keep taking steps forward, little one."

Shush walks forward a little.

I take her hand. I want to encourage her. "I'm proud of you, Reba."

She gives me the longest hug. "We're almost home, Sugar Mae Cole."

I'm not sure about that, but I keep my mouth shut.

"I've still got lots to work on," Reba says as the bus pulls up. Shush is shaking from the noise. Reba turns to me. Her eyes look sad. "Do you like it at Lexie's?" She shakes her head. "I already know the answer."

She climbs on the bus. Shush and I watch it go.

Almost.

It's a big word for me.

I feel it everywhere.

Almost home.

Almost happy.

Almost changed.

Almost, but not quite.

Not yet.

Soon, maybe.

I'm hoping hard for that.

37

THE PHONE AT Lexie's rings at 8:25 a.m.

I hear her say, "Well, no she's not. No, she doesn't live here. Just a minute, Sharon. I'll ask her daughter."

I run into the kitchen.

"Sugar, did your mom know she was supposed to be at work at 7:30?"

"She knew," I whisper.

Lexie's back on the phone. "She's just delayed, Sharon. She doesn't have a phone. Yes, I know. I'm sorry . . . of course I will."

She hangs up. "Now I'm calling the shelter and we're going to get to the bottom of this."

Reba doesn't get up that well sometimes . . .

Or she didn't make it back.

Nobody is answering the phone at the shelter.

My mind is going crazy.

"Maybe something happened," I say.

Lexie shakes her head. "I'll try again."

I pick up Shush and go into the tangerine room. I bury my face in his good fur. I'm getting a stomachache from worry. I look at the dollhouse. The mother doll is in the kitchen. It's so perfect, it's irritating.

It's her first day of work.

Couldn't we just get a break on her first day?

I take the father doll and throw him across the room.

Then I see Lexie standing in the doorway.

I run to get the father doll. "I'm sorry, I don't know why I—"

"I've thought of doing that myself," she tells me.

I gulp. "Did you talk to the shelter?"

"Something is wrong with their phone. I can't get through."

I feel this fear sitting on my chest. Something bad has happened to Reba. I know!

Just then, Shush starts going crazy running around the room. He jumps up at the window, whining.

"What is it, boy?"

He's pawing at the window.

"Do you have to go? You have to go out the back. Come on."

But Shush won't move.

I try to pick him up but he jumps away.

"What's with you?"

He's whining louder. I pick Shush up and take him out back, but he won't go in the backyard. He runs through the kitchen to the front door.

And now he does something he's never done before.

He barks!

I'm not kidding.

Shush barks again!

"What is it?" I shout.

Lexie throws the front door open.

And there is Reba, sitting on the porch with her face in her hands.

Shush runs to her, barking. She touches his chin. "Are you barking for me?"

"What happened?" I shout.

Reba shakes her head.

"The bus was late and then the next bus broke down and I asked a woman if I could use her phone and she said no and I didn't have change to make a phone call, and I walked here in these shoes . . ."

She takes them off; she's got bleeding blisters on her feet.

"Oh, Reba!"

"I tried to get there."

Lexie bends down. "Yes, you did. I'm calling Sharon right now."

"The whole world has a phone," Reba whispers. "Except me."

"Lots of people don't have phones, honey." Lexie puts her hand on Reba's shoulder. "Don't let this bad morning stop you. You've got so much to build on."

Reba grabs Lexie's hand. "I don't deserve your kindness."

I look at Reba and she looks at me. I sit down next to her.

Lexie's saying she's going to call Sharon, but I don't think she should do that. Reba should call for herself.

I take Reba's hand. "You remember that time I came home from school crying because I didn't get into the school play?"

"I remember."

"You remember what you told me?"

She touches the little silver bell necklace, and it's like she gets some kind of power from it. She sits up straight and goes all-out Southern. "Why yes I do. I told you to not worry about one bad audition, but ask for another one."

"And I got the role of the lead armadillo."

"I was so proud of you on that stage. Lord, I was bursting." She smiles brave like only a Southern woman can.

Let me tell you about my mother.

She gets kicked around a lot, but she gets up, too.

She's King Cole's daughter, and that's close to being royalty.

"Well," she says to Shush, "if you can bark, I can, too."

She straightens her shoulders and gets herself up.

She calls Sharon and asks for another chance.

She slaps bandages on her blisters.

She brushes herself off and marches off to the Sweet Spot. Actually, she's limping, so Helen drives her.

Shush and I stay back in the kitchen.

"You barked," I mention to him. "You sounded totally ferocious. Am I going to have to change your name?"

Shush looks at me.

"I guess you've been holding it in for a long time, huh?"

Shush puts his paw on my arm and sighs.

x x x

"I've got a big question to ask you, Dana."

Dana Wood sits back in her ugly brown chair and

smiles like she's used to big questions.

"Do you think Reba is going to get all better?"

She doesn't look down or take a sip of coffee to think or any of that. She looks at me straight on. "I think your mother loves you very—"

"That's not what I asked."

She holds up her hand. "Let me finish. That kind of love can be transforming. Do you understand?"

"It can help her change."

"That's right."

"She wants to change real bad."

"And that can be like a key that unlocks a door."

I understand about locked-up things. I've got another big question. "What if Mr. Leeland comes back again?"

"When people want to make big changes in their lives, they need to understand what's healthy for them and what isn't."

"You're talking to Reba about this, right?"

Dana Wood smiles. "I can't tell you what we talk about, Sugar. That's confidential."

"But you're covering the big change stuff, right? I mean, you're not missing any major life points, because sometimes with Reba, you've got to really ram it home for her to get it."

Dana Wood leans back in her chair. "I'm going to ask you to trust me on this, Sugar."

Trust isn't a natural gift that I've got.

I trust you.
I mean, I think I do.
I want to, but I'm not sure I can.
Inside my heart I wonder
if I can trust anyone really.
I trust you.
Sort of.
Maybe I don't know you well enough
to trust you.
Maybe I shouldn't even try.
But I will . . .
Try, that is.
At least, I think I will.
When I was little
I thought trust was just a word.
But it's more than that.
It's a promise.
Do you promise I can trust you?
If you do, then maybe I can.
I promise I will try.

38

WHEN I GO to pick up Merlin for his walk, he doesn't want to get up from the porch. Shush tries to nudge him, Puffypoo and Greg whine in his face, but this old dog just sniffs and lies there. Mr. Cockburn sits next to him, so sad, patting him, then Merlin closes his eyes and stops breathing.

Mr. Cockburn breathes deep and closes his eyes. "You did good, old friend."

I don't know what to say.

Shush and Puffypoo get quiet. Greg throws back his head and yelps.

Mr. Cockburn's face is all red. Finally, he says, "I'm going to call the vet to come get him. Will you sit with Merlin?" He gets up slow and walks into the house.

I've never sat with a dead dog before. I want to say something good to seal the moment. A fly lands on Merlin's nose and stays there.

"Well, Merlin, you're going to the last roundup." I heard a cowboy announce that in a Western. "You're the first dog I ever made money on and don't think I'm not grateful. We had some pretty good walks—slow, but decent, and except for that time when you scared the soup out of Laney Diver's cat, you've been a good dog. Going after that cat, I guess those were the days, huh?" I feel my eyes getting moist. "I didn't know it at the time, but I loved you, boy."

Merlin doesn't respond, for obvious reasons. Mr. Cockburn comes back out. His eyes are wet.

"You're a good girl, Sugar."

He hands me a twenty-dollar bill, which is more than I ever made in a day while Merlin was alive. I feel funny taking the money, but I get over that.

"Thanks for letting me share this life-and-death moment with you, Mr. Cockburn."

He looks like he might want to take the twenty back, so I just do the best thing a helping person can do—I shut up and sit there with him.

All the dogs are quiet. Then Dante walks by.

"Will you hold the dogs for a minute?" I ask him.

He comes up on the porch. Mr. Cockburn covers Merlin with a blue sheet, sits down, and puts his hand on the lump that is Merlin.

Dante shakes his head sadly, and I walk across the street to Lexie's, and get one of her candles from the front porch and a matchbook from the Opa! Greek Diner. I bring them to Mr. Cockburn's porch and light the candle.

"For Merlin," I say.

The peach scent rises up and the flame stays steady in the pink glass holder.

Mr. Cockburn nods. "Looky here, Merlin, what Sugar's brought us." Then he lowers his old head and cries.

x x x

Dog walking isn't the same without Merlin. All the dogs miss him, especially Shush, who stops by Mr. Cockburn's house every day looking for his friend. Mr. Cockburn doesn't seem the same. He doesn't come out on his porch nearly as much, and when he does, his smile is smaller, but Shush always trots up the stairs to give him a hug.

Joonie says we should get Shush one of those helper dog vests, so people know who they're dealing with from the start, but I think they know. Sometimes caring is so strong, you can't help but know.

I want to do something for Mr. Cockburn. I can't

drive him someplace to get a break or give him money or anything like that, but I can give him a fresh perspective.

"What's your favorite color?" I ask.

He looks up. I can tell color isn't a big part of his life.

"I mean, do you like green or blue or yellow or—"

"Purple," he says, and you could have knocked me over that this gray-faced old guy would have that kind of stuff inside. "When I was young, I had me a purple shirt that I got in France. Nobody else had one, and when I wore it, I felt like a king."

"Mr. Cockburn, would you like me to paint your front door purple?"

He laughs. "Well, that might be kind of showy."

"Yes, sir, that's the point."

x x x

I take care to fill in the cracks, and Joonie sands the door down good after I show her how to do it. The best leaders don't stand there watching, they get in there and help. Dante knows about painting, and he's getting the brushes ready. I picked a rich purple paint, the kind a king would have on his front door.

Mr. Cockburn sits in his chair with Shush on his lap, saying, "I hope the neighbors don't get upset."

"Helen's going to want this," Joonie says. "You won't be alone."

And sometimes you just have to get out there with a bold color and shout to the world who you really are. I take the paintbrush in my hand and dip it in the royal purple paint, and from the first brush of paint on that old door, I feel like something is changing.

"My Lord," Mr. Cockburn says, "that is glorious."

I give it two coats and kill myself getting the edges neat. It takes some time to dry. Neighbors stop and stare.

"Cockburn," a man shouts, "what's gotten into you?"

Mr. Cockburn laughs. "Well, I do believe it's new life, Boylston. You should try it sometime."

"I'd like a purple door," an old woman says.

"This is the girl you want to talk to." I head down the steps smiling. "But she and her team aren't done here yet." He grins at me. "Sugar Mae Cole, you need to sign your work."

What is he talking about?

He points to the door. "Down there in the corner, sign your name."

Dante opens the can of white paint we used on the door frame and hands me a small brush. I kneel down and write *Sugar Mae Cole* and underline it with my signature whoosh.

That looks fine, but it needs something more. I laugh, and above it I write, *Yours very truly.*

"Now it's done," Mr. Cockburn says. "I want to pay you."

"You can pay me for the paint, sir, but not for the work. It's my thank-you."

Shush purrs.

x x x

I show Reba the door, and she says I've taken gratitude to a new level. The whole block is talking about it, and we paint two more doors purple, one tangerine, and another one bright red. We are making decent money, too, but more than that we're helping people live bold.

"Front doors have power," I explain to Puffypoo's owner. "They're the first thing we walk through, and when they're shouting boldness, it does something to people."

Helen gets her door painted royal blue, and her shoulders go back every time she walks through it. She's ready for anything. I wish I could paint a door for Reba, but she needs to get her own place for that to happen.

Reba is working hard at the Sweet Spot, shoving all she's learned about sweetness right in the customers' faces. Mildred, the waitress, stays sour.

"I've only got two hands, and they're both busy now," Mildred tells a customer.

"Sit down, take a load off, and wait your turn," she snarls to someone else.

And Reba runs over and makes things right, asking about their children, and saying the Sweet Spot is so happy they stopped for refreshment along life's busy path.

"I think I was meant for this job," she tells me as Mildred harrumphs and waddles out with an order. "I've got so many ideas. My head is bursting!" But riding two buses twice a day is getting her close to bursting, too. She needs to find a place to live that's closer to work that she can afford. She can't find anything, though. Sometimes Helen drives her back to the shelter. They're becoming good friends.

The word gets out that the Sweet Spot is taking sweetness to a new level and all of that is making Reba nervous, as more customers show up expecting the world.

"I'm not sure I'm really up to this," she tells me.

She's in her room at the shelter. It's Monday, her day

off. I go over to be with her on Mondays because we don't get to see each other as much as we planned. She's exhausted at the end of the day.

People don't understand how tiring it is to be sweet.

"Someone suggested we open earlier," Reba tells me, "but I don't know, Sugar . . ."

She puts on a green shirt she got at the Salvation Army. It's amazing what people give away. It has a ruffle around the collar.

"You look real pretty, Reba."

Her hands go up and down, which means she's feeling helpless. "Sharon keeps asking my opinion on things—should we add more to the menu? What color should we paint the place? This is a lot for me. I don't want to tell her the wrong thing."

"Sharon wouldn't ask if she didn't trust you."

Reba stomps her foot. "Why would she trust me?"

"You're smart. You know how to make things nice."

She sits down on the bed and puts her head in her hands. "It's hard for me to be out front for people and always smiling, when I've been through what I've been through."

I sit next to her. "You're doing really good, though, Reba."

She shakes her head. "But inside sometimes I'm not."

That scares me.

"Inside, sometimes, I don't feel like I'm strong."

I don't know what to say, except, "Doesn't everybody feel like that sometimes?"

"Not everybody shut down the way I did."

I don't want to have to say it, but she's not giving me any choice.

"Miss Reba, you wrote me that note saying you were back and you were going to get better and when you need reminding, I was supposed to do it. Okay, I'm doing it."

I yank her up and get her standing in front of the mirror above her dresser. "You see that pretty lady there? That's my mom. And she's got grit. She's even got the shirt to prove it."

Reba gulps.

"King Cole said, 'You don't listen to the voices inside you telling you you can't be much. You just tell them to take a hike.'" I wait for that to sink in. "That's on page thirty-seven of his book," I add.

"What chapter?"

"Chapter five—'A Life of Kicking Butt.'"

Reba nods and stomps her foot again, but in a different way.

"You know more about sweetness than any person on this earth, maybe," I tell her.

She nods. "Well, that's true."

I'm trying to remember some of the things she told me. "You told me a kind answer turns away anger. And that being kind doesn't mean you're blind."

She smiles. "When you're nice, it doesn't mean you've got lice."

I stand there like a coach telling the team to go out there and win the big one. "So, you go out there, Reba, and get up in people's faces. You show 'em what it means to be sweet."

x x x

I am getting good at painting doors and rooms. I write Mr. B an e-mail about it and he writes back.

> You know, I've always wanted to have a red wall in my classroom.
>
> Something bold to wake kids up. Maybe I should do that.

I write him back.

Do it, Mr. B!

I would do anything to paint it for him, but he's in Missouri and I'm in Chicago. I tell him to pick a red with a little brown in it, because it will stand the test of time.

I feel like this whole summer has been a test for me. I love being at Lexie's in the pink room, but it still isn't fully home exactly because Reba isn't there.

Sometimes I feel like the time here is clicking away.

Then Joonie tells me, "I think Helen and Reba have figured something out." Her braces gleam. "And the Zid-donian Council has approved the measure."

GIVEN THE FACT THAT HELEN, JOONIE, AND CHANDLER MERMAN WERE LEFT FLAT BY HARGROVE MERMAN III AND NEED EXTRA INCOME . . .

GIVEN THE FACT THAT THE MERMANS HAVE AN EXTRA ROOM, WHICH DOES NEED SOME REDECORATING, BUT IT IS A ROOM NONETHELESS . . .

GIVEN THE FACT THAT REBA COLE, SUGAR'S MOTHER,

NEEDS TO LIVE CLOSER TO WORK SO SHE CAN WORK HER MAGIC ON THE MASSES . . .

WE, THE ZIDDONIAN COUNCIL ON FAMILY AFFAIRS, HEREBY DECLARE THAT REBA COLE SHOULD RENT THE MERMANS' SPARE ROOM, WHICH WILL ALLOW HER TO WALK TO WORK AND ALSO ALLOW HER TO SEE HER DAUGHTER MORE, ALLOWING MORE HEALTHY FAMILY INTERACTION, WHICH IS WHAT ZIDDO IS ALL ABOUT.

WITNESSED THIS DAY OF AUGUST 4TH

THE WOOZ

It is undersigned by the Great Company of Elders and Butterbutt.

I hold the paper, feeling about a hundred things. I try to get up the courage to say the next part. "This is great and all, I'm just worried. What if Reba messes up again?"

Joonie sits down. "We're not expecting perfection."

"But what if she messes up big?"

"We'll work with it, Sugar."

39

FROM THE FIRST slosh of blushing rose paint on the wall, I know I'm in the zone.

I don't put more paint on the roller than I need. I don't have drips or leaks. My arms are strong and I can roll the paint straight and blend it to the top of the wall, where I cut in the corners with the paintbrush like Lexie taught me.

I give it two coats and do the trim in white. I paint the tired wooden desk yellow and the scratched wooden bed white.

I'll tell you what—a twelve-year-old who knows how to paint a room knows about power.

It's humid, so the paint takes longer to dry, but now it's done and you wouldn't believe this room. Helen gets daisies and puts them in a pitcher. Joonie shoves the yellow desk against the wall. I put Reba's box of thank-you cards on the desk and her pens in a Sweet Spot mug, ready for graciousness. I hang sheer white curtains I bought for two dollars at a garage sale. I put up a butterfly picture in a painted yellow frame. The brown rug doesn't match, but that's okay.

Reba's been looking down for so long, this gives her a big reason to look up.

Total cost: $23.37

Joonie sighs. "I should never have given up this room."

Reba shouts from downstairs, "I simply cannot wait another minute!"

I shout back, "Don't open your eyes until you get inside."

Helen, Joonie, and Chandler bring Reba in. "No cheating," Chandler says.

I grin. "Okay, you can look."

This room we're in, it brings sunshine to my mother's face.

"Will you look at this!" she says.

Reba touches the walls, she touches the bed, she runs like a little kid and looks out the window. She sits at the desk. "This is perfect for writing my cards. Thank you. Thank you from the—"

She straightens her shoulders; she shakes back her hair.

I know why. This isn't a day for crying, this is a day to feel great.

Helen says, "You breathe in these colors, my friend. This is you now."

Reba can't speak just yet, but she does nod.

"Is she sick?" Chandler asks.

Tears burst from her eyes. "I'm happy!"

Chandler can't cope with this and heads downstairs.

X X X

Waking up in a blush rose room is doing big things for my mother. And having her across the street? It's not as weird as it sounds. She comes by Lexie's every morning to give me and Shush a hug.

It's sweet—and I don't use that word lightly.

Reba is working like a thing on fire. She unpacks her sweetness every day and finds something new. There is newness everywhere, from doors to walls, to Mr. Cockburn getting a new dog from the shelter named Boris. Sometimes I just start laughing for no reason.

I don't see the next monster rising up. There are no ripples in the water whatsoever.

40

I HAVEN'T SEEN Dante much because he's working on this big project in a park. I decide to take Shush, Puffypoo, Greg, and Boris and go over there. I'm just crossing the street with Shush in the lead when a silver car rounds the corner and the horn blasts.

I freeze. *Oh no.*

Mr. Leeland waves and sounds the horn again.

I wait for Shush to freeze at the noise, but he doesn't.

"This isn't good, Shush." He cocks his head and looks at me.

Mr. Leeland stops the car, and that's when Shush jumps up, barking. Not cute barking, either. This dog is growling mad, pulling at the leash.

"Easy, boy."

He's barking like his life depends on it.

Mr. Leeland pulls the car to the curb and says, "Good morning."

"Hi."

Shush is trying to attack the car.

"What's the matter with him?" Mr. Leeland asks.

I'm not sure, but then I know. "He's trying to protect me."

Shush is showing his little teeth and growling at Mr. Leeland.

"Protect you from your father?" Mr. Leeland laughs.

"Guess so."

Puffypoo rises up and Greg starts howling.

Mr. Leeland turns off the car and tries to open the door, but the dogs are there growling.

He looks down at them and stays behind the wheel. "How come you hate me so much, Sugar?"

I was just planning on walking to the park. I didn't expect this kind of a morning.

I gulp. "I don't hate you." I shake my head and look at Shush—his ears are back, and his body is stiff, ready to pounce. "Good boy. It's okay." I rub his neck.

Mr. Leeland says, "Don't you believe in new starts, Sugar?"

"Sometimes."

"Well, that's why I'm here."

"Reba went to work," I tell him.

"I've got the address. She and I talk, you know."

Obviously.

"I'll take a run over there. Maybe we can all have dinner tonight."

I don't say anything.

Mr. Leeland looks at me with his big brown eyes. "You know, I couldn't stand my pop when I was growing up. I can tell you, not giving him a chance hurt me."

He starts the car, backs halfway down the street, which you're not supposed to do, runs over a flowering bush on the corner, and heads toward the Sweet Spot.

I don't have a phone to call Reba, and I won't make it back to Lexie's in time, so I head to the park with my killer dogs. I sit on a bench and give them treats.

"Thanks, you guys. You did good. All of you."

I look at Shush. "And you were the most ferocious of all."

Shush licks his mouth.

X X X

I walk over to the garden in the park where Dante is working. He's lifting big rocks out of the soil.

"We didn't know they were there," he tells me. "We have to get rid of them or the plants won't root deep and be healthy." He looks at me. "What happened?"

I shrug.

"Is your mom okay?"

"I don't know."

He looks at his hands. "I never told you this, Sugar, but that guy I'm named after—Dante—the guy who wrote about hell and stuff . . ."

"Yeah?"

He looks down at the big rocks. "He wrote about leaving the things you love and how that's one of the hardest things in life to do."

I look at this boy covered with park dirt. "Why did he write about that?"

"I don't know. I guess it's because he was a great man and understood stuff that hurts."

x x x

Reba is humming as she takes the sweetie pies from the bakery box and puts them on a plate in Joonie's kitchen. Helen is making tea, and Chandler looks disgusted.

There's a knock at the door. And my heart sinks. I just know.

My father comes walking through the door with two bouquets of flowers. He smiles his Hollywood smile and bows. "Ladies, with my compliments." He gives one to Reba and one to Helen. He puts a box of chocolates on the table. His eyes look funny.

"Now you're talking," Chandler says, and takes off the box top.

Mr. Leeland gives Reba a too-long kiss and I know. It's over. All we built here. It's done.

Mr. Leeland goes to sit down and almost misses the chair. He's drunk.

I sit here like I'm made out of rock. I feel my face get tight and my jaw get hard.

I feel the stone go into my neck and down my arms.

I am the stone girl.

You can't reach me.

I won't let you.

You can't hurt me anymore.

Nobody can.

41

REBA'S NOT PAYING attention, but Helen is.

"Sugar, let's go into the other room."

"You got any beer around here?" Mr. Leeland says.

Reba pauses. "It's morning."

He laughs and heads to the refrigerator. No beer.

Helen takes my arm. "Come on."

I walk out with her into the living room.

"You're drunk," I hear Reba say.

"So?" Mr. Leeland says back.

"I'm sorry this is happening," Helen tells me.

"It's happened before."

"Your mom is stronger now."

I'm not so sure.

"I don't appreciate you coming here drunk!" Reba shouts from the kitchen. "I thought you told me you stopped."

He laughs. "Well, I did, baby, and it just wasn't any fun."

"What are you doing, Lee?"

A crash. Helen and I run back in. A chair is on its side by the back door with the leg broken.

"Get out," Helen says to him.

"I'm here to see my family," Mr. Leeland tells her.

"This is my house. I'm telling you to leave."

Mr. Leeland picks up another chair, and now Chandler makes a big run at him from behind, shouts a war cry, and pushes him down. Mr. Leeland is on his face, moaning.

"Stop it!" Chandler screams. "Stop it! Stop it! Stop it!"

Reba walks over to Chandler, puts both hands on his shoulders, and says, "It's all right. Thank you." She looks at Helen and there's something new in her face. "I'm sorry about this."

And maybe it's that she's filled herself up with good things, maybe she's just sick and tired of being treated bad, but my mother looks at the lump on the floor that is Mr. Leeland and instead of standing by her man, she stands on him.

Right on his back.

He groans a little when she does that. Reba isn't all that big.

"Get off me, woman," he mumbles.

"I'm not quite ready to do that, *darling*."

Joonie laughs. Of course, it's not her father lying there.

"First item, dear, and do pay attention because I'm only going to say it once." Reba's voice rises in full-out Southern disgust. "If you want any kind of contact with me or Sugar, you will need to be sober. Stone cold sober. Is that clear?"

He mumbles something.

She digs her heels into his back. "I can't hear you!"

He moans again.

"You get up from the mess your life is in, Leeland. Do you hear me? You start living right, boy. You stop gambling and wasting your life and wasting my time with your hollow promises. I'm sick of your excuses. You be a man, sir, a man of honor. I'm not settling for anything less."

"Whoo-hoo," Helen says.

"Don't forget the money he borrowed from King Cole," I whisper.

"And you pay back every cent you borrowed from my father!"

"Come on, baby, you know I love you."

"If this is love, I'll take a pass."

"You know you don't mean it," he says.

"Go get some help, then we can talk. And by the way, spending time on a riverboat gambling is not getting help."

She jumps off his back, yanks him to his feet, pushes him out the door, and throws the flowers he brought out, too.

"I'm keeping my flowers," Helen says.

Shush pads in from under the table. Butterbutt sits there on her perch by the back door. The two animals stare each other down. Animals don't blink, so it's hard to tell who wins.

Reba's back in the kitchen now, and she looks straight at me and in front of everyone says, "I want you to trust me again, Sugar. I'm going to make up for the lost time. You'll see."

Helen goes back to making tea, and Reba finishes putting out the sweetie pies.

"Does this mean we're a family?" Chandler asks.

Shush and Butterbutt glare at each other.

"We're a . . ." Helen starts. "What are we?"

"A unit?" Joonie suggests.

Reba giggles. "A gaggle?"

"A team . . ." Helen says.

Joonie is looking up appropriate words on her phone. "Band, clan, herd, pack, gang, group . . ."

Chandler grabs a sweetie pie and walks out. "I'm sorry I asked."

"Maybe we're a mob," I say.

"That's cooler," Chandler says from the other room.

Helen pours the iced tea into glasses. She puts a sugar bowl on the table, milk, and packets of sugar substitutes.

Please. In my mind there is no substitute.

42

DEAR SUGAR,

Now that the school year is about to start I want to wish you a great seventh-grade year. I hope you'll show your teacher some of your writing.

You know what I learned this summer? I had all these things I thought I was going to do—organize my files, organize my life—but my mom was sick and that took most of my energy. Then two days ago, I did the craziest thing. You know that awful wall of mine across from the windows—the one filled with scratches and gashes from seven years of extreme teaching. Well, I painted it red. It's beyond fabulous, if I do say so myself. When I finished painting I twirled Claus in the air. Even though he's a rubber chicken, he appreciated the moment.

You go out there, Sugar Mae Cole, and make a colossal difference.

Thanks for the inspiration.

Mr. B

Mr. B—

I would like to see your red wall someday. That desk of yours was pretty ugly—maybe you should paint it red, too? But don't slam Claus down on it until it's totally dry.

Thank you for everything you keep doing for me. I hope they're paying you enough at the school.

Yours very truly,

SMC

Dear Sugar,

They're not paying me nearly enough, but kids like you make up for it.

TGB

I'm working on a piece of writing for my new school. We're supposed to take a word and define it and use an example out of our life. My English teacher, Mrs. Nord, sent a letter to all the kids in her class and asked us to do this before school even started.

ALMOST HOME

by Sugar Mae Cole

Home isn't always a place you picture in your mind
With furniture and cookies and music playing and people laughing.
Home is something you can carry around like a dream
And let it grow in your heart until you're ready for it.
Losing things helps you appreciate when you find them again
And finding things gives you hope that when you lose things
It might not be forever.
Once, long ago, a girl lost her home, but she didn't lose her dream.
She hung on to it as the wind kept trying to blow it away,
But that just made it stronger.

So now she has keys and walls of many colors
And people around her who think she's
something.

x x x

It's the first day of school. I look at Shush and deliver the news.

"Dogs can't come to school."

He jumps up like we're going somewhere.

"I think it would help to have dogs at school, but education doesn't always get it right. I'm sorry." He cocks his head listening. "I'm going to be gone all day, but Lexie needs guarding."

"I really do," Lexie adds, smiling.

"And Mr. Cockburn says Boris needs someone to play with, so you can go over there and be a role model. Okay?" I scratch his good head. "We've been through a lot of change together, right? And we can handle this one."

I pick him up and give him a hug. He lays his head against my shoulder.

"Yes, you're the best dog in the world. And that girl Jenny who had you, she loved you, but not as much as me."

Shush wags his stump of a tail.

"Okay, I've got to go be a seventh-grader."

That sounds so old.

"You knock them dead," Lexie tells me. "Come on—I'll walk you out."

Mac comes, too, and just as we're heading out the door, Reba waves and crosses the street. "You have the best day now, you hear?" She hugs me with strength.

Mr. Cockburn salutes me from his porch. "Kick butt!" he shouts.

"Yessir!"

Mrs. Boylston shouts, "They're lucky to have you."

Helen starts up the car and Joonie puts a sign in the back window for all the world to see.

PROUD PARENT OF THE WISE ONE OF ZIDDO

Helen sighs. "What happened to 'proud parent of an honor roll student'?"

Joonie makes a face. "Helen, you're so much more than that."

Dante runs over. He's going into eighth grade, but he never turns down a ride.

He smiles at me. "You look good."

I look down. "You do, too."

"Hmmmm . . ." Joonie says and gets Chandler in his seat belt.

Helen shouts, "And we're off."

"Way off," Joonie adds.

Puffypoo, Greg, and Boris bark. Shush whines at the door, and Lexie lets him out. I wave at everyone.

It's awesome to have a crowd cheer you on.

x x x

I turn my "Almost Home" poem in to my teacher, Mrs. Nord. I stand by her desk, hoping she'll read it in front of me, and she does. A big smile spreads over her face.

"I love this, Sugar."

I grin back. "I've got more."

"I'd love to see your writing."

I stomp my foot. *I can definitely work with a person like this.*

But this school I'm at, it needs fresh paint on the walls.

I ask Mrs. Nord, "Did you ever think of getting bolder colors in here?"

She nods. "Every day."

I picture the red wall Mr. B is going to be looking at all year. I see him leaning against his desk, twirling Claus his rubber chicken.

I sent him an e-mail last night.

You should get an award for being a teacher.

He wrote back.

I've been waiting by the phone.

And I'm able to say, I miss him, but I'm here now.

It's okay here.

More than okay.

It's a good place to grow, and I plan to do that.

I'm working hard to have a good life.

You don't need fancy things to feel good.

You can hug a puppy.

You can buy a can of paint and surround yourself with color.

You can plant a flower and watch it grow.

You can decide to trust people—the right people.

You can decide to start over and let other people start over, too.

Every morning Reba tells me, "You go out there, Miss Sugar, and show 'em what it means to be sweet."

"Yes, ma'am, I will."

It's a natural gift that I have.

JOAN BAUER
writes about
Almost Home

I WAS ON a plane to New Zealand to visit my sister when I first "heard" Sugar's voice in my head; I felt an urgency to write down what she was saying. Who was this girl? Where was she? On the street, that much I knew, but not on her way home. No, this girl had lost her home. What was that like? What kind of a girl was she, who had influenced her, where did the strength come from that would help her survive? The first lines I wrote were these:

I'm in front of you, but you don't see me.
I'm behind you and you don't much notice or
hear my voice.

With those words, she had me. I had to write her story, and I realized that sometimes home, a real home, is a thing you have to search for with all your heart. This girl's got a heart big enough to carry her through.

The doogs

were crying!!!